also by kim addonizio

What Is This Thing Called Love, Poems

Dorothy Parker's Elbow (edited with Cheryl Dumesnil)

Tell Me, Poems

In the Box Called Pleasure, Stories

The Poet's Companion (with Dorianne Laux)

Jimmy & Rita, Poems

The Philosopher's Club, Poems

little beauties

a novel

kim addonizio

Simon & Schuster
New York   London   Toronto   Sydney

SIMON & SCHUSTER
Rockefeller Center
1230 Avenue of the Americas
New York, NY 10020

SIMON & SCHUSTER and colophon are registered trademarks
of Simon & Schuster, Inc.

For information about special discounts for bulk purchases,
please contact Simon & Schuster Special Sales at
1-800-456-6798 or business@simonandschuster.com

Book design by Ellen R. Sasahara

Manufactured in the United States of America

10 9 8 7 6 5 4 3 2 1

Library of Congress Cataloging-in-Publication Data

Addonizio, Kim, 1954–
Little beauties : a novel / Kim Addonizio.
p. cm.
1. Obsessive-compulsive disorder—Fiction. 2. Teenage pregnancy—Fiction. 3.
Teenage girls—Fiction. 4. Fetus—Fiction. I. Title.

PS3551.D3997L58 2005
813'.54—dc 22
2005042564

ISBN-13: 978-0-7432-7182-0
ISBN-10:   0-7432-7182-3

for my daughter, Aya—
queen of my heart

acknowledgments

I am indebted to Josephine Yu for telling me her story; driving me from dinner to my hotel, she planted the seed for this book. Susan Browne and Jessica Barksdale Inclán read the manuscript and helped me understand my characters more fully and find my way to the unfolding of their experiences. Lisa Glatt has been a friend and inspiration as I made the transition from poet to novelist. Robert Specter supplied endless love and endless lattes during the writing. I am also grateful to my agent, Rob McQuilkin, for every little thing he does; and to Marysue Rucci at Simon & Schuster, who is a dream editor.

Two books helped me to enter the world of an obsessive-compulsive: *The Boy Who Couldn't Stop Washing* by Judith L. Rapoport, M.D.; and *Stop Obsessing! How to Overcome Your Obsessions and Compulsions* by Edna B. Foa, Ph.D., and Reid Wilson, Ph.D. Some of the chapter headings are borrowed or adapted from the latter book.

part one

RULE #1: Shower after emptying the trash.

ONCE I was a professional princess. At age four, I was chosen, out of a very competitive field, to represent my preschool in the Palmetto Avenue Neighborhood Association Parade as Princess Moonglow. At seven, I was both Fairyland Angel and Sassy Star, while fulfilling all my elementary school duties and also my required household chores. I was twice crowned the Vegetable Princess, or at least the princess of a few green growing things, like cabbages. I was Miss Teen Broward County at the tender age of fourteen. At fifteen, I stood in a white cowboy hat in front of a car dealership, in wind that whipped the colorful pennants around and nearly tore the petals off the roses I was holding, and tried to pretend I wasn't wearing a bikini and five-inch heels in front of a bunch of grown men. I smiled. My mother, Gloria, ducked into the driver's seat of the red Mustang convertible I had just won for her, showing her legs as she did so, diverting some of the male attention her way. A salesman patted my ass as she was adjusting the bucket seat. That day I was Freddy's Ford Cowgirl. But then I threw in my sash.

Now I'm thirty-four, and I have just become Employee of the Month: August at Teddy's World. I guess I still have a thing for titles, in spite of my official retirement. I've made Employee of the Month in every job I've had. That's a lot of jobs. We're talking double digits here. Fourteen, to be exact. Start with your left thumb and go down to your pinkie; then your right thumb to right pinkie; back to your left thumb, forefinger, middle finger.

Stop at what is known as the ring finger.

Right now Gloria is trying to reach me on my cell phone. I'm not supposed to have my phone on while I'm at work, but someone might call me—someone besides my mother—and I want to be there if that someone needs to talk to me, if he needs to tell me that he misses me and wants to come home. So there the phone sits, vibrating crazily on the counter of Teddy's World, behind a pile of *Poker Babies*. *Poker Babies* is a book with photographs of babies who look like they are playing cards, with thought bubbles above their heads saying things like "Deuces wild" and "I'm calling your bluff." It's stupid and precious, two qualities that have made it a steady seller in baby stores across the country. Here in Long Beach, it's doing really well.

My phone has stopped vibrating; Gloria's name has disappeared from the display. She'd probably be happy to see I've made Employee of the Month at Teddy's World. I have to admit it gives me a little charge when customers glance up at the color head shot Tim took earlier in the summer. This was before he took leave of our marriage, which immediately drove me into a high-end salon in Belmont Shore for a savage haircut by someone named Linda, who was not, despite her name, very pretty. Average looks, extreme poise, zero personality. And definitely no talent with the scissors. Linda's talents, whatever they were, were not on display. "Can't you make it a bit less poofy on top?" I asked her, and she said, haughtily, "Then it will have no shape at all," and continued to hack away. When she was done, the hair I could once sit on lay all around me like a bunch of straw, and I wanted to lie down in it like a sick horse.

So all in all, considering recent events, I really needed to make

Employee of the Month, a bright spot in a bleak stretch. Never mind that there are only two of us. A couple of weeks ago I suggested to Marlene, my boss, that having an Employee of the Month would make her look like a caring businesswoman, someone who appreciated her workers, so she said okay. She said I could be first, since I've been here longer than the other girl.

Usually, by the time my winning smile appears inside a frame on the wall, I am on my way out. I'm gone before the glass gets dusty. But I like Teddy's World. I've been here since May, among the jungle mobiles and snap-on pajamas, under the miniature model train that endlessly circles the store on its tiny tracks, the plastic engineer touching his cap in greeting, the smiling plastic children strapped in and waving. When Marlene hired me, I thought, What could be better than baby clothes, fresh from the manufacturer, the babies themselves safely quarantined in BabyBjörn carriers or in strollers, or, safer still, in the wombs of their soon-to-be-mothers? Plus, these mothers are easy marks, and I get commission on the larger items.

I smile at a pregnant woman looking over the cribs in the back. I leave my post at the counter and lead her down the rows. I can tell that when I'm done with her, she is practically going to buy the store. She looks about five months gone, maybe six. I'm pretty good at guessing by now.

"Marvelous!" she says, when I show her how to click the rails up and down on a maple hardwood drop-side crib.

"Adjustable-height metal springs," I tell her. "And it can be used as a bed when the baby's older." I load her up with the drop-side crib, the matching armoire with removable shelves and bar, and the marvelous nursing station—a gliding rocker with matching ottoman, five fabric patterns to choose from. She's torn between Angel Blue and Delicate Flower. While she's debating, I stroll over to a grandmother and help her pick out bonnets and booties, a lacy christening jacket, two teething rings, and a plastic cow that plays Mozart. I ring up Grandma and then write up the order for the nursing station; we don't keep those in stock.

"So, Delicate Flower it is," I say. "Excellent choice."

"It feels kind of silly," the woman says doubtfully. "I mean, I can just sit on the couch and nurse, right?"

"Motherhood is tiring," I tell her. "You should pamper yourself."

"This is my first," she says. "Do you have children of your own?"

"Not yet," I say, feigning a regret bordering on bereavement. "One of these days."

"I'm so excited," she says, pulling out a Platinum Visa. "I just can't wait. We're going to have three. I'm going to breast-feed them all, of course. Children need their mother, right from the beginning."

She looks around Teddy's World, like she's already planning what to buy for the next two. She doesn't even notice I'm Employee of the Month; she's too busy being Expectant Mother of the Century. She looks about thirty, fresh-faced and happy. Right now she is free and unencumbered. Soon she will have an infant fastened to her breast like a polyp, clutching fiercely at her expensive blouse. She will be held prisoner by a screaming baby, standing on its rubber mattress and rattling its crib bars. By the time she is done having her family, birthing and coping with three children, she will look like a hag. The fabric of the nursing station will be faded and worn. She will just shove a bottle of formula in the last baby's hands and stick it in its crib, and she will glide back and forth in the nursing station rocker, longing to end it all.

"That's fifteen hundred and twenty-nine dollars," I say, taking her card.

A heavyset woman comes in, pushing a twin stroller. I don't

know if these babies are twins or not. The babies all look alike to me, blobs of clay with glittering eyes and little smashed-in noses and wet lips.

I lean over them and breathe in their gauzy, milky smell. "So beautiful," I say. I kneel down and wave a clown rattle at the twins. I look up at the mother with tears in my eyes. I can do tears on a dime. Not really tears, just a moistening of my eyes that makes it look like I'm on the verge, like I'm overcome with emotion. Judges used to fall for it all the time.

"You are doubly blessed," I say.

"Yes, I am," she says. She thinks I mean it, and I can tell she's actually happy to have the two of them, and for a minute I'm jealous.

Then I notice it, under the new baby smell: something rancid, something I don't want to get too close to.

When the mother leaves, I notice the stroller wheels. They roll across the pale blue-and-pink swirls of the store's carpet, and I see the tracks, thin, sinuous parallel lines between the rack of overalls and the shelves of stuffed animals, lines that snake back and forth and cross each other until the colors of the carpet are barely visible. And, I mean, I just knelt down on that carpet. In shorts. Which means I've gotten it on my skin—the oil and dirt from the streets, the smashed gray gum and spit and crud from the sidewalk.

Teddy's World is starting to get contaminated.

Contamination is why I had to leave my managerial position at Liquor Barn, why I did not last at Real You Salon or Dr. Woo's pediatric dental practice. I didn't make it as a telefundraiser for Save the Earth, or as auto parts inventory control clerk for Nissan. I washed my hands, over and over, but they would not come clean. Each time I quit, I removed my name in block capitals and my smiling head shot from the wall, and I walked out and threw them in the nearest trash can.

I don't want this to happen at Teddy's World. I need Teddy's World right now.

I'm supposed to be on Zoloft, but I've kind of stopped taking it regularly. My therapist, Sharon, told me it was important not to stop my medication, or our work together, just because Tim left. Stay with it, she said. Do your homework. Practice the Calming Breath. Break a rule.

The Calming Breath is simple. You breathe in and count to three, and then let out the breath as slowly as you can while trying to relax. The trouble with this is that I only seem to be able to do it when I'm already sort of relaxed.

Which I am not, at the moment.

The rules are posted at home, on the refrigerator, with a Teddy's World magnet. They are also posted in the laundry room and taped inside the bathroom cabinet. This is—I mean, was—for Tim's benefit, not mine. I know them by heart, since I made them up. There are currently thirty-seven items on the list. There used to be eighty, before I started with Sharon. I was down to twenty-four when Tim left. After that it seemed necessary to add a few again.

Without rules, all is chaos and darkness.

"Excuse me," a girl says, and I look up from the crazy lines, suddenly realizing that she's been standing there for at least a minute without saying anything.

"Do you have any music boxes?" she says.

She looks like she's in high school. High school kids these days dress like toddlers. She's wearing a teeny white ribbed top with a Hello Kitty on it. Her glossy dark hair is done up in pigtails; her skin is dewy as a baby's. Below the shirt, her bare stomach is a soccer ball, the belly button popped out. If I were still at Liquor Barn and she came in for cigarettes I'd definitely card her. If she walked into Liquor Barn, I'd be watching her to see if she tried to take anything. She has that look.

"Music boxes. No. We have jack-in-the-boxes. We have toys that play music. We have teddy bears and pigs and dolls you can wind up and listen to, but we don't carry music boxes."

"Oh," she says, a little, disconsolate "oh." Like she'd really expected to find a music box, like she needs it right now.

I look past her at the lines on the carpet, pulsing and glowing. I blink, trying to make them go away.

"Are you sure?" she says. "Miss McBride? You look different," she says.

She's looking at my picture behind the counter. Of course I look different; the woman in the picture has long hair. She is married. McBride is my married name, and I never liked it. It was too much like McDonald's. McJob. McMarriage, McBride. Still, it was better than Rose. I was born Diana Rosen, but one day Gloria changed it. She got the idea that Rose would be a better pageant name, so she dragged us right down to the county clerk. Gloria is half Jewish, on her father's side, but from that day on we were Presbyterian, which she explained was a more refined and forward-looking religion. We never actually went to church or anything.

"Please just call me Diana," I say.

The girl crosses her arms. Her nails are short and painted a grape color, and the polish is chipped, and I can tell she doesn't even care.

No wedding ring, I notice.

"Do you have anything that plays—" She "dah-dah-dahs" a tune, Beethoven's "Für Elise."

"That's a popular one. We have a few things that play it."

I lead her over to a shelf of stuffed animals. "These are the musical ones." I know I'm walking over the lines on the carpet, but I try to tell myself it doesn't matter. I walk on the streets every day, so what's the difference?

She cranks up a teddy in overalls. We have all kinds of teddies—pink teddies in diapers or long dresses, plaid teddies, the classic teddy—naked, brown-furred, and, if you had one as a child, irresistible. I had one, which got lost years ago, and I bought another one from the store at an employee discount.

The girl holds the teddy to her chest and closes her eyes. Her face scrunches up, and I'm afraid she's going to cry.

"Why that song?" I ask.

She opens her eyes. "I had a music box once, that played it."

"So you want one for your baby. How lovely!" I click on the enthusiasm. "When are you due? Looks like any day now."

"No," she says.

"No, what?" I hold my smile.

"I don't want this baby," she whispers.

"Of course you do. Babies are such a precious gift." I wipe my hands on my shorts. "A gift," I repeat.

"Fuck that," she says. "I don't want this fucking baby."

"Of course you don't," I say. Why argue with her? I totally understand.

"I'm giving it up as soon as it's born. To be adopted." She looks at me defiantly, like I'm going to say it's such a tragedy, or something.

She's clutching the teddy to her. Its music loop has stopped. I look into its painted glass eyes. I used to look into the eyes of my childhood teddy, Ginger, and see infinite love. This one just looks at me, though. That's how they all are now. Today's teddies look out only for themselves.

I curl my toes in my sneakers, thinking, My feet are safe, inside the sneakers, inside the socks. Thinking, I want to go home and shower.

"Want me to ring that up?" I say.

"No." She puts the teddy down. I turn away to see if there are any actual customers who need my help. But by the time I get back to the counter, she's picked it up again and followed me.

"Sorry," she says, setting the teddy on the counter, not looking at me. She stares at the cover of *Poker Babies,* a drooling kid in a diaper clutching an ace in its fist.

She'd do terrible in a pageant interview, I'm thinking. Eye contact is crucial.

Just then, Marlene comes out of the back room with Kelly, the new employee. "Yes, yes," Kelly is saying. "I'm sorry. I know. I'll try."

Kelly will never be Employee of the Month. I will win, every time. Kelly is not perky. She has eczema on her elbows, and her outfit is hopeless: a shapeless dress that is totally the wrong color for her and doesn't hide the ugly flowers tattooed on her arms.

Eczema is a form of dermatitis. It often runs in families. Luckily, it can't spread.

"Diana," Marlene says, "be a dear. When you're done helping this customer, run up to Starbucks and get me a double Mocha Frappuccino."

The outer layer of human skin is made up of keratin-producing cells, which are pretty much dead. They slough off continually. So even if I can't catch Kelly's eczema, I don't want to get too close to her. I move back as she comes around the counter.

"Skim Frappuccino, right?" I say. If I take my break now, I'll have time to get home, shower, and stop at Starbucks on the way back. Teddy's World is just a longish walk from the apartment. I'll tell Marlene there was a big line at Starbucks and that they got the order wrong the first time.

"That's my gal." Marlene loves my ass. She says I have managerial potential. Potential and I are old friends; my pageant career was built on it. Mostly what I have now, I think, is failed potential. No way I'm going to say this to Marlene, though.

I ring up $24.95, plus tax, for the teddy in overalls. The girl digs into a big denim purse, scrounging for balled-up bills, taking them out and flattening them onto the counter one by one with agonizing slowness.

"Do you want a bag?" I ask her, practically grabbing the last five dollars from her hand. We have pink-and-blue striped paper bags with handles, showing a teddy clutching a bunch of balloons, each balloon holding a letter of TEDDY'S WORLD. We have gold tissue paper, and gift wrap with teddies or balloons or birthday cakes and hats. We have flattened boxes that can be put together in a matter of seconds. All these are in neat cubbyholes behind the counter, giving off a faint gassy odor.

"No thanks, I'll carry it," she says.

Marlene comes over and pushes the clipboard on the counter across to the girl. "Sign our mailing list," she says. "We've got lots of wonderful sales coming up."

"Uh, no thanks," the girl says.

Marlene picks up the clipboard and kind of jabs it at her. The girl looks at Marlene. Marlene smiles. "Please, dear," she says. "Sign it." Marlene can be kind of intimidating, if you don't know her. Kelly is obviously scared to death of her, another reason Kelly will never get ahead here; she doesn't project an aura of confidence.

"*Act* like a winner," Gloria used to say, "and you will *be* a winner."

"Whatever," the girl shrugs, and uses the pen, attached to the clipboard with a blue shoelace, to write down her information.

"Diana dear," Marlene says. "Get me a slice of lemon bread, too. No, don't. Oh, go ahead." Marlene is watching her figure, as she puts it. She watches it get to a certain size, and then she starts throwing up her lunches in the bathroom.

I nod. I can keep it together. I can. Marlene takes a snowsuit off the Hold rack—there are people who buy snowsuits in Long Beach, presumably to give their babies a head start on the slopes of Mountain High or Snow Summit. She whisks it over to the second register.

For an instant, giving the girl her change, I catch her eye, and neither of us looks away. If we were both younger, in the dressing room for some competition, I'd be sizing her up and weighing my chances. Thinking maybe she could take me, with a certain kind of judge. She's pretty, the dark-haired, big-eyed, sad kind of pretty that sometimes edges ahead of a blonde no matter how soulfully you play "Amazing Grace" on the accordion, or how brilliantly you smile like you're about to swoon with ecstasy. It's a fact of life, you get used to it.

"Good luck," I say. "With the adoption and everything."

She turns, and heads for the door to the street. I watch the stuff on the carpet swirl around her. Most of it settles back, but I notice a little gets on her shoes. I can see it very clearly, just like I can see that I am in more trouble than she is.

2.

JAMIE Ramirez walks out of Teddy's World and stands for a minute looking up and down Second Street, at all the girls her age with tank tops and flat stomachs and no problems. They peer into store windows, drag each other inside, and come out laughing hysterically. They stand on corners, licking ice cream cones suggestively when boys in long baggy shorts walk by. They can hardly speak for giggling. They double over as though they've been punched in the stomach and stagger back against a light pole. Their lives are hilarious.

"You're not like other girls," Kevin had said when they first got together. "You don't, like, laugh all the time."

"Nothing's funny," Jamie had said. She was a senior in high school then. She hadn't applied to any colleges, because she was sick of school. She worked behind the candy counter at one of the AMC theaters in the mall. She was sick of work, too. Over and over she had to say, "Can I serve the next guest?" which made her feel freakish and fake.

Kevin had ordered a giant tub of popcorn and a Dr. Pepper and Junior Mints, and invited her to a party at a house he lived in with some other guys. At the party, Kevin had said, "I know what will cheer you up," and led her up some narrow stairs to his attic room. It wasn't the first time Jamie had had sex with a boy, and like the other times, it had mostly hurt and she wondered if it was her fault.

She watches a man and woman, leaning toward each other over their frozen blue margaritas at an outdoor table at Taco Loco. They lean in and kiss in slow motion, with a kind of self-consciousness—like they're being filmed, like any minute the other patrons are going to burst into smiles and applause. Jamie had liked kissing Kevin. She had liked kissing all the boys she slept with. Sleeping with them was the price she paid for getting to feel their breath on her neck, their soft tongues exploring her molars. While they kissed her, she stared unblinking at their closed eyes, in case they ever opened them.

Another couple walks by, arms around each other, hands in each other's back pockets. It's a law of nature, Jamie thinks. When you feel fucked up, everyone is happy. When you are alone, the world is an ark. You are a bizarre animal, one of a kind, and they are sailing off as the rain comes down harder and the water starts rising over your knees.

At Kevin's house, the bathroom was down the stairs and around a sharp corner, a white room with one magazine page Scotch-taped to the wall—a blonde wearing large breasts and no pubic hair, exposing a glistening vulva that looked like it had been given a coat of pink lip gloss. The floor was warped, and there was never any toilet paper on the metal holder. This is where Jamie always peed and washed up after sex with Kevin, where she once dripped a small droplet of mentrual blood on the dirty tiles that no one wiped away, where she later crouched over the toilet with morning sickness. This was where Kevin stood in the doorway and said, "I'm outta here," looking not at Jamie peering up through her sweaty bangs but at Naked Magazine Woman, as though she was the one he was breaking up with, running away from, joining the Coast Guard to forget her quarter-sized blush-enhanced nipples and fuck-me-now smile.

Jamie hopes that Kevin has to scrub the bathroom toilet on his ship with a toothbrush. She hopes he gets washed overboard by a giant wave, then bitten in half by a shark. By the time his shipmates throw him a life preserver he will be just a torso in the water.

She decides to go to the beach to clear her head. The only other place to go is home to her parents' house. Her father will be propped in front of the TV. Her mother will be in her studio painting fairies and unicorns, with some crappy New Age music floating out on the fumes of Nag Champa incense. If Jamie is lucky, the beach won't be crowded. She will be able to sit and look at the offshore oil platforms in peace and quiet.

Stupid, she is saying to herself as she crosses Ocean Boulevard. Spending all that money on a stupid stuffed bear.

She had lied to that lady in the store. She never had a music box like that when she was growing up. Her friend Leila had owned one. You opened the lid and two ice skaters, a boy and a girl, tracked around in a circle while the cylinder turned in the clear glass box, playing "Für Elise" in pure, sad notes. It was like fairy music, Jamie used to think. She had coveted the box and Leila knew it, but Leila never gave it to her. Jamie had always wanted what Leila had. Parents in the entertainment business, a big house, a Platinum Visa with a five-thousand-dollar limit when she graduated from high school.

Now Leila has gone off to college, to NYU. Jamie misses her so much. She just needed to hear that song again, to make her feel like Leila is close, when she is really so far away. They haven't even talked on the phone for two weeks now. Leila is busy with classes and new friends, while Jamie is wandering around aimlessly, buying shit she can't afford and doesn't want.

Leila is going to be a dancer, as graceful as the girl skater in her tiny gold costume, a boy circling faithfully behind her. Jamie

is going to be lying in the hospital like a stranded whale, screaming, feeling like she has to shit a hot toaster oven.

This is how Leila's mother had described what Jamie's
mother calls the miracle of birth. Leila's mother offered to
arrange an abortion, but Jamie's mother wouldn't hear of it.
Jamie's mother, Mary Wagner-Ramirez, is Catholic. She believes
in the Gift of Life. She doesn't believe in Raising the Baby on No
Money and with Your Poor Father on Permanent Disability.

"Adoption," Jamie's mother said, "unless you're planning to
move out and raise it on your own."

This last option sounded too fucked up to seriously consider.

Jamie had settled on thinking of this baby as a tumor. For
nine months, it would grow, but it wouldn't invade the rest of
her life. In just a few days now, the doctors will cut it out.
Nurses will whisk it away, and she will be cured.

So why buy it a fucking teddy bear?

She reaches the beach, sits down, and pushes off her flip-
flops, digging her feet underneath the hot sand. There's a long
sidewalk that cuts across the beach, parallel to the shoreline. Bi-
cyclists and Rollerbladers and power-walking old women whiz
past her. Just watching them is exhausting.

She sits the bear upright in the sand, and it falls over. She digs
a little hole for it and sets it inside.

Let the new parents buy it shit, she thinks.

I'll keep it for myself.

Keep what?

The bear. Not the baby. I am definitely not keeping the baby.

It's your baby.

Jamie picks up a handful of sand and lets it run out onto the
legs of the bear, the overalled knees with red patches on them.
She imagines some sweatshop worker in Malaysia or somewhere, leaning over pair after pair of teeny identical overalls for
twelve hours straight in a hot, noisy room, the needle hammer-

ing in the stitches. All over the world, people are doing work that sucks.

She remembers burying her father once, up to his neck, then him doing the same to her. It was scary to lie under all that sand, to feel like she might not be able to push her limbs through the heaviness and get out. Her father could do it—he would rise right up—but she needed him to dig her out a little before she could stand. The sand clung all over, shiny on her skin. She ran into the ocean to wash it all off. Sand weighed down her bathing suit bottom. Her father would lift her underneath her arms, and dip her in and swish her around, and she'd beg him to do it all over again.

Now her father is a brain-damaged freak.

Shit happens, and then you die.

A freighter goes by slowly on the horizon. At least Kevin, in the Coast Guard, will be going somewhere. She's glad she's not with him, but it would be nice to get out of Long Beach.

She pushes some more sand into the hole, completely covering the bear's legs. Maybe the lady at the store will let her return it, but maybe not. Maybe she should just bury it.

3.

STELLA shifts restlessly in Jamie's uterus. It's hard to relax, when Mom is so keyed up. Take it easy, Mom. Everything's okay. I'm snug and cozy in here. Crank up that music again. Stella gives Jamie a little elbow jab, just to let her know she's awake.

I'm your baby, Stella says. *Mom,* she calls. That is, she thinks it at her.

"What?" Jamie says, looking out to sea.

I chose you, Stella tells her. I'm not going to let you just hand me over to somebody else. I've come all this way to be with you. I've traveled farther than the farthest star, and believe me, that's really, really far.

Jamie puts both hands to her stomach.

Stella listens to the whooshing sound of Jamie's blood. It's better than the teddy bear music. She really liked the music, though. Hearing it in Teddy's World, she had called to Jamie, *Want that.* Music is something she's looking forward to hearing more clearly, when she gets out there.

It's okay that Dad won't be around. Bon voyage, Kevin. All she needs is Jamie.

Stella knows everything that's happening to Jamie, and everything she's thinking. She knows her mother can't really hear her, that it's more of a feeling Jamie gets sometimes. When

Jamie first realized Stella was there, when she got drunk and kind of let herself fall down Kevin's stairs, hoping to dislodge the baby, Stella floated toward her in a dream. I forgive you, she told Jamie, and meant it.

Stella had loved Jamie as soon as she saw her. Jamie was at a party, doing bong hits. Her jeans were embroidered with flowers she'd done herself. She had glitter on her shoulders, and she was sitting on a sagging couch watching a silent *Star Trek* rerun, not talking to anyone. Around her, girls were laughing and falling down drunk. A boy was throwing darts at a poster of Britney Spears tacked on one wall. Jamie hunched forward, staring at the uniformed Klingons giving Captain Kirk some kind of advice, or maybe an ultimatum. A boy passed the bong to Jamie and held the match to the bowl while she sucked up all the smoke in the glass tube.

Sometimes, Stella thinks, you just know.

Mom, she calls again.

"Fuck you," Jamie says. "I can't wait to get rid of you."

4.

RULE #27: Wash any bedding that touches
the floor.

WHEN I get home from Teddy's World, I check the machine. There are four messages. "This is Gloria," my mother begins, as though I might not recognize her voice. Or maybe she simply doesn't want me to mistake her for anyone named Mom or Mother, Mumsy or Mama. Anything that smacks of maternity.

"Diana. Please don't do anything," she says, and hangs up.

"Whatever that means," I say to the machine. What would I do? I already ruined my hair. Thinking about it makes me want to cry, but I don't. Crying is for losers. In competitions, when I didn't make the cut, I smiled. I counted backward from eleven, silently, over and over. In those days I was beguiled by numbers, instead of bars of soap.

First a counter, then a washer and cleaner.

You've also got hoarders and checkers. You've got repeaters, arrangers, pure obsessionals. Ever get a tune stuck in your head? Some people, it drives them nearly insane.

After the next beep she says, "This is Gloria. The bastard," she says, meaning Tim. "Men are scum. God damn them! God damn them all to holy fucking hell!" Only the second call, and she has already moved into hysteria. Gloria is good at hysteria, the way some people are good at math or cards. She throws fits. In public. I can't tell you how many times in my life I have edged away from her, slowly, while she screamed at a shoe salesman or grocery checker. The thing is that they never seemed to mind. They would look abashed, and then apologetic, and then they would get several more boxes of shoes or call for someone to help her carry stuff to the car.

These were men, of course. Gloria is also good at men, a trait I did not inherit. My father, whoever he was, must have passed on to me some predisposition toward confusion in that department. The only men I ever charmed were people who didn't know me personally, like pageant judges and guys passing me in cars. And Tim. Now the charm is gone. The bloom is off the rose. The rose is in a vase without water, its petals browning and shriveling.

"Be brave," she says. "You'll get through this. I'll help you." There's a pause, some fumbling, and I hear what must be the ice in her glass, clicking against her newly implanted teeth. It's the cocktail hour in Northern Virginia. The cocktail hour starts at breakfast with a vodka-and-grapefruit, tapers off by mid-morning, and resumes again about two in the afternoon. "Has he called you yet?" she says.

He might, I think, if you weren't tying up my phone all day with your messages. He just might. Tim often changes his mind about things, and it's only been forty-six days since he left, so it's not out of the question. Tim and I were married for twelve years. Twelve, a good number. I always liked twelve, the two curved over next to the one like a swan, protecting it.

"Fred and I are going to dinner," Gloria says, in a normal voice. "Call me tonight. We'll be back by ten."

Ten was bad, I remember. The one standing next to a hole it might fall into.

Last night I called Gloria, and finally told her what I'd been hiding from her for weeks, that Tim had moved to an apartment in Los Feliz. "Fee-lace?" she said. "Spell it." I did. "To happiness?" she said, translating the Spanish.

"It's less than an hour from here. It's in L.A."

"You married beneath you."

"Come on, Gloria. You always liked Tim."

"You can do better."

"I love Tim," I said.

"Walk away," she said, as though he hadn't already done exactly that.

And Tim isn't a bastard. I understand why he left me. I hate it, but I understand: I am hell to live with. If I could leave myself, believe me, I would be packing right now.

I take off my white scoop-necked T-shirt and then my shorts, careful not to let the shorts touch the floor. I lay them over an arm of the couch. My sneakers came off as soon as I hit the front door, like always.

"This is Gloria," begins her third message. "One more thing. You were a winner. Tiny All American Photogenic. Miss Veteran's Day. The Express Auto Parts Princess. Remember your personal introduction for National American Miss? You said you saw yourself making the world a better place. Now look at you," she says, like she can see me, standing in my socks and underwear in my living room, turning in little circles with my eyes closed, waiting for her to stop.

"You had such a promising career," Gloria says.

This is how my career began: In 1968, on the basis of my personality, beauty, and natural appearance, I was awarded a blue ribbon at the Pasco County Fair in Dade City, Florida. I was six months old. Gloria had saved up her tip money from Dot's Diner for weeks. She had gone without things she needed, like shoes for her aching feet, in order to drape her precious girl in a white silk christening gown. She took the day off and, because she didn't own a car, she hitchhiked down State Road 52. I rode on her hip, wearing nothing but a diaper. She walked backward on the road's gravel shoulder, the gown neatly rolled up in her purse. In her version of events, she trudged all the way to the fair in the broiling Florida sun while the air-conditioned cars whizzed by, while I wet my diaper through and wailed. In her version, that is, she sacrificed everything to make something of me, while I did my damnedest to thwart her.

"What happened to my little princess?" she says. "Did she go on to compete in Miss Teen USA? She did not. Did she try for Miss Florida, or even Miss Jacksonville? No, she did not. She threw it all away."

"Oh, shut up," I say to the machine. I feel tired and itchy. I can see dust floating on a shaft of light through the diaphanous blue curtains Tim bought after I complained about the old ones, which were heavy and soiled.

"Fred wants to go down to Florida this winter," Gloria says, sounding conversational now. "I told him no. Too many painful memories."

In Gloria's mind, I was scouted by film agents and movie producers, when all we did was go on toddler cattle calls. And I'm convinced that some driver stopped to pick us up, that day I won my first pageant. Mothers and babies do not get passed by, especially when they are beautiful. The world stops for beauty. I bet it stopped for Gloria that day, when she was nearly thirty but still looked like a teenager. Now she is sixty-four. You'd think no one would look twice, but you'd be wrong. Some beauty peaks early, like mine did; and some, like my mother's, defies certain notions about time and age. Of course, it helped that her third husband, the one before Fred, specialized in a few cosmetic procedures.

"I think you should go on some auditions," she says. "Listen,

Fred wants me to get off the phone now. I'll talk to you tomorrow. Bye-bye."

She misses the cradle trying to hang up; I can hear her fumbling with the phone, and then Fred saying "Oh, for Christ's sake," and then she's gone. Fred came in from the living room, from the leather recliner with the heated seat that vibrates and moves from a three-quarters reclined position to full horizontal. Gloria's husband is not what you'd call an active senior.

I go to the machine and erase the messages. But the memory of her voice hangs in the air. Straighten up, baby. Smile.

The last call is a hang-up that could be Tim, though why would he call here if he thought I was at work? To hear my voice saying "You've reached Tim and Diana"? To make sure I was out, so he could sneak back for more of his stuff? He left most of it here, like he was only packing for a short trip. Little by little, things have been disappearing. A week after he left, I came home from work and his weights and bench were gone. The next week, several DVDs and videos were missing from the shelves under the TV. There's still a lot here, though. A lot of things a person needs if he's really going to start a new life.

Maybe he wanted to start fresh. I can understand that.

Tim and I started fresh often. Once the contamination found me at work, it started to follow me home. Eventually—after a year, sometimes two—we'd need to move. New apartment, new furniture. Every time, I thought things would be different.

I peel off my bra and underwear, pick up the shorts and T-shirt, and head for the shower. Just a quick one. I make sure the water's good and hot, and unwrap a hotel soap. I lather myself twice, then twice more, starting with my hair, then moving down, against the flow of the germs traveling up from the floor. Usually it's three and three, but I need to go back to work. I can towel my hair dry in a hurry, now that most of it's gone. I put on fresh underthings. Then I'm back in my same clothes—

which is against Rule #34, and makes me start to itch again, but Marlene will notice if I show up wearing something different.

I wipe the steam off the mirror to redo my makeup. I'm an expert at makeup. At Real You Salon I did high school girls for parties and proms. I did brides and maids of honor and a female comedian who thought somebody from HBO might show up at her performance that night. I made them all look great, and they gave me big tips and bought a ton of products. But a hair stylist's station was next to mine, and eventually the dead hair that fell from her scissors started to get to me.

Maybe I could call Marlene and tell her I fell over a broken sidewalk on my way to Starbucks, or got knocked to the ground by a Rollerblader. I'm in the emergency room, I'll say. It could take hours.

Go, I tell myself in the mirror. Go back to work.

I sit down on the toilet lid.

Before Tim left, I was actually improving. Tim had said that if I didn't get better, he was going to leave. Last fall he found me a psychiatrist, Dr. Freitag, who put me on Anafranil and then sent me to Sharon for behavior therapy. I got better, but not fast enough, I guess. For example, if I got up at night to pee, I didn't shower. That was a big deal. I broke Rule #42. I'd flush the toilet, wash my hands three times, and go straight back to bed. Major victory. Sharon thought so, anyway. I crossed Rule #42 right off the list.

Tim's razor is still on the sink. If I open the bathroom cabinet, I'll see his Edge Shaving Gel, his Opti-Free contact lens solution. *And* his lenses, in their plastic case. Most of his clothes are still in the closet. I imagine him unshaven, his eyes smaller behind his glasses, wearing the same shirt day after day, and I think: He'll come home. He can't live like that for long.

I haven't taken my meds for five days now.

Go back to work, I tell myself.

When I felt like this, Tim would always say, You'll be okay, Diana.

No, I won't, I'd say.

Will.

Won't.

Will.

Won't.

Will, will.

Won't, won't, wont.

You were fine last month, he'd say. It was all fine. The new job, the place, everything was cool.

Well, it's back.

Well, make it go away again.

This is how we went around and around about it, and never got anywhere. I'd be more normal for months at a time, or nearly—it's not like I could stop totally, but I'd manage to cut down drastically—and then it would start up again with a vengeance.

I go into the bedroom and call Marlene, and tell her how I was struck with heavy period cramps halfway to Starbucks, how I rushed home bleeding to change my clothes. I am such a good liar.

"I'll be back as soon as I can," I say. "With your Frappuccino."

"Poor baby," she says. I wait for her to say, "Take the rest of the day off," but of course she doesn't.

"I'll get everything done. The Tommee Tippee sippy cups," I say, like ordering them is my purpose in life.

I've been squirming out of my clothes while we talk. I undress before the blank eyes of the teddy I bought from the store. It's propped on its shelf across the room, like a catatonic in a ward. If it could shake its head sadly, it would. Diana, it would say. Take your meds. Call Sharon. Don't even think about reinstating Rule #42.

"Oh, I ordered the sippy cups," Marlene says. "Not to worry."

"Maybe I should stay home," I say.

There's a pause at the end of the line. "Well," she says finally. "If you really think you need to."

"I can come in early tomorrow."

"You know how much I count on you. You are such a lifesaver, Diana."

No kidding. Not to be immodest, but Teddy's World might fold without me. Marlene is not the best businessperson. I am very organized and efficient. No one, seeing me on the job, would ever imagine what kind of shit goes on in my head.

I decide to put my dirty clothes in the washer and take one more shower, and then I'm going to change the sheets and crawl in for the rest of the day, even if she orders me back to work.

"All right," Marlene says. "I suppose Kelly can handle things, just for an afternoon. You take it easy. Take a Motrin. I know it's awful."

"You have no idea," I say.

5.

JAMIE can't face going back to the store, trying to return the teddy bear, seeing that lady she said "fuck" in front of. She pulls it out of the sand and brushes it off the best she can. She cranks up "Für Elise" again and thinks about hanging out with Leila in high school. Being in Leila's room with the canopy bed, leaning over the balcony that looked out on the backyard pool, eating the ham-and-Gruyère sandwiches the maid prepared and brought in for them on a little tray. The maid's name was Graciela. She was from Guanajuato, and her English was bad. She tried to speak Spanish to Jamie, but Jamie couldn't understand. Jamie's father is from Mexico, but he came to L.A. as a child, with his fruit-picking parents. He probably would have understood the maid, but not been able to talk to her. Leila, whose origins are Hungarian, Polish, German, and Latvian, can speak Spanish better than anyone in Jamie's family except Jamie's grandparents, who are dead now. Leila, Jamie thinks, will be able to carry on the Mexican language and culture. Leila also knows how to make tamales.

Jamie watches the oil pumps go up and down, like mechanical chickens pecking for seed, like mechanical penises entering robot vaginas in a porn video. She wonders if robot porn exists; there seems to be a fetish for everything on earth. Kevin had shown her a catalogue of magazines and videos for pee freaks.

A NO WAR FOR OIL bumper sticker is plastered on a nearby trash can. Maybe Kevin will have to go to Iraq. The Iraq war is supposed to be over, but everyone is still fighting. Maybe the Coast Guard, though, is safer than the Army or Navy or Marines. Jamie's not sure what the Coast Guard does, exactly, except look for people who fall off their yachts.

Two weeks ago, on the phone, Leila had suggested suing Kevin so he would help pay for the baby. Leila is always convinced that litigation is the answer to everything, because it made her parents rich; they are entertainment lawyers.

"He doesn't have any money," Jamie said.

"So sue his parents," Leila said.

"I've never even met his parents." The idea of Kevin having parents is hard to grasp. He was never a little kid, never yelled at his dad or refused to do chores. He has always been twenty-two, a boy in a dirty group house with a futon bed and a broken Lava Lamp. Jamie can't picture him in a uniform.

"You are such a dope," Leila had said.

Leila would never be in this situation. She would have just snuck off and gotten an abortion, without telling her parents. Jamie had told her mother, like an idiot. She was raised to tell her mother everything. When she got her first period, she dutifully called from the school nurse's office to relay the news. When Jamie got home from school, there was cake and champagne on the table, under a mobile of tampons, their cottons dyed different colors, dangling from the light fixture by their strings. When Jamie let a boy French kiss her, her mother took her to a gynecologist and got her a prescription for Estrostep; Mary Wagner-Ramirez wasn't a perfect Catholic. If only Jamie could have remembered to take the stupid pills every day, instead of forgetting half the time. If only she'd asked Kevin to use a condom, but she didn't feel she knew him well enough. It was too embarrassing to raise the subject. They'd only known each other a few weeks when she got pregnant.

The baby kicks hard, twice. Jamie imagines its tiny feet, then blocks out the image of anything resembling a human. The baby has tentacles, and bulgy eyes. The baby is a freak. Someone will take it home and love it, but not her.

There's another sharp pain. Not a kick this time. A cramp. She doubles over, and it passes.

Two girls Rollerblade by, decked out in their blading gear. Knee pads, elbow pads, wrist pads. Tiny jean cutoffs, neon orange and green halter tops, and no helmets. They jerk along slowly, just learning, almost falling. They laugh. Rollerblading is hilarious. Jamie hopes they land on their heads and end up like her father. They will speak only a few words, mostly the wrong ones. They won't laugh, just look confused and frustrated, and then whistle through their teeth, meaning that another word they wanted has dropped through a hole in their brain.

The girls glance her way, their eyes passing over her like she's a rock, a piece of wood, a dead bird. They are probably best friends. They will get out of high school and move to L.A. together, where they will meet interesting guys with wallets full of credit cards and condoms.

"Fuck you," she calls to them. They haven't gotten very far past her. One grabs the other and they look at her, really look at her this time.

"Well, fuck you too," one of the girls says. "What's your problem? Bitch."

"Pregnant bitch," the second one adds.

They both laugh, and roll farther down the path.

6.

RULE #48: Blow into a cup before you use it (to make sure there's no dust in it).

I CARRY my clothes to the washer, push them in quickly, and close the door. Dirty clothes live in the washer until it's full. That avoids having them in a laundry basket, which I'd then have to clean. The laundry room is also where the shoes live, shoes that have touched the filthy streets. It is impossible to wash certain kinds of shoes, so containment is the next best thing.

In the laundry room I can't help seeing Tim's black Rockports, his flip-flops, his New Balance tennis shoes, his two pairs of Tony Lama cowboy boots—snakeskin and elephant—lined up on the plastic sheeting. He must be wearing his Nikes, day after day. Rotation of footwear is Rule #4. Tim is no longer following it.

I started the rules after moving out here with Tim, when we were first married. I left Gloria's apartment in Virginia—she hadn't met any of her husbands yet, so it was just her and me—for a tiny, grimy one-bedroom in Silver Lake that never seemed to get clean enough no matter how many times I mopped and dusted and swept. At first there weren't too many items. Tim was kind of a neatness freak anyway, so it seemed pretty reasonable to him. Gradually, over the years, the list got longer and the rules got stricter. Still he did his best to follow them, and like I said, we were down to hardly any when he left. One by one I crossed them off. Now I realize he is doing the same with our wedding vows: crossing out the "sickness" and the "till death" stuff. Soon he will cross out "love," and "cherish," and after that he'll find a new girlfriend, and "forsaking all others" will disappear beneath a solid black Magic Marker stroke. Tim will make love to her in his bed in Los Feliz, their clothes carelessly strewn on the floor, their shoes touching the fibers of the bedroom rug, and afterward they will sleep on sheets stiff with their sweat, tiny pieces of their skin flaking off like dirty microscopic snow.

I close the door to the laundry room and go to shower off Teddy's World once again. I don't feel like changing the sheets in order to get into bed, so I put on fresh clothes instead. I go to the kitchen to throw out some roses I bought the other day. I bought them because Tim used to get them every Friday, bringing them back from Sunrise Cut Flowers at the downtown Farmer's Market. I bought them to torture myself, and they are doing the job.

The night Tim proposed was full of roses.

We were in a restaurant in Adams Morgan, a neighborhood in Washington, D.C. A band was playing loud Cuban music, and we leaned close to each other, shouting into each other's ear, over our tapas of miniature filet mignon and fried plantains and yuca root patties. When an old bent twig of a woman came by with her overpriced roses, Tim bought two reds and a white. He drank an entire pitcher of beer, except for the glass I was taking little sips of, since I didn't really drink. When he noticed my glass he finished mine, too. Then he started tearing apart the roses, putting petals on my shoulders, down my blouse, on my eyes. He put one in my open mouth, and I felt his thick index finger press against my tongue.

We had known each other three days. He'd walked into the cocktail lounge of the Arlington Marriott, where I worked, and after I served him several beers he insisted that I take him on a late-night tour of every monument in the Nation's Capital. We held hands at the Lincoln Memorial and kissed at the Jefferson. We lay on the grass by the reflecting pool looking up at the Washington Monument: 555 feet, 896 steps to the top. We lay there until morning, and then went to breakfast in Georgetown, and somehow we couldn't part company. I called in sick to work two nights in a row.

"Diana Rose," he said, that third night. "Be my McBride."

It was the easiest title I ever took. Besides, Tim wanted to go to California, across the country from my mother. Tim's Irish, and he wanted to become an American citizen. I was afraid that if I didn't marry him, I'd never see him again. He would find another girl to marry, and fill her mouth with flowers—a girl named Lily, or Violet, or Iris.

"You're fucking adorable," Tim said. "You should always be covered with roses." He put a white petal on his tongue, and stuck his tongue in my red-petaled mouth.

Which, of course, I thought was kind of unsanitary. But there were too many happy little hormones salsa-dancing through my bloodstream for it to bother me. I was twenty-two, and Gloria was driving me crazy. Serving drinks at the Marriott wasn't exactly fulfilling. I had attended George Washington University and then the University of Virginia and finally Fairfax Community College, each stage of my academic career less promising than the last, and had not managed to get a degree. I had credits in psych and English and accounting. I had, really, no idea of what I was supposed to be doing. Besides my mother, Tim was the first definite thing that came along.

The roses on the kitchen table are yellow and insanely cheery. They are beautiful and doomed. I throw them into the kitchen compactor and turn it on, listening to them being smashed flat. I fill the black vase with scalding hot water and soap. I look at the dish sponge and I'm suddenly afraid to touch it, even with my dishwashing gloves on, so I just leave the vase in the sink and peel off the gloves.

I go into the bathroom and look at my bottle of Zoloft, touching shoulders with Tim's Valium in the cabinet. He got the Valium in Mexico, and took it sometimes to sleep, or just to get a little buzz. I've never taken one. I've only ever taken drugs when they were prescribed by doctors. Tim has gone through all the Vicodin I had left from my dental surgery in April, I notice; the bottle's there, but it's empty. He will come back for the Valium, I know it.

I tap one out and break it in half and swallow it with some saliva.

Now what? I wait a minute at the sink, but nothing happens. There is a tiny, threadlike hair in the sink, the blond comma of one of Tim's beard hairs. So maybe I was right about the hangup; he called to make sure I wasn't here, then snuck in to get something while I was at work this morning. He must have stood here—in his dirty Nikes, I bet—looking into the mirror, rubbing at his short beard and wondering whether to wait another day to trim it. Automatically I turn on the faucet, but as soon as the hair slips down the drain I want it back. It's gone, though. I look at the bottle of pills with my name on it, at the instructions in capital letters, telling me clearly that I should be taking one every night at bedtime. But I have a better idea.

The idea is this: To hell with it.

I'm tired of trying to take my medication and doing homework for my therapist, like a little kid in school—practice this, confront that, visualize some other stupid thing. I tried. I drove all the way to Sharon's office in Santa Monica, every two weeks. I went back to Dr. Freitag when the Anafranil made my heart race, and started on the Zoloft. I stayed with it, even though it gave me insomnia and made me feel even less like sex than I usually did. I got the list down to twenty-four items, even though it was really, really difficult. It took months of hard work, and then Tim left anyway.

I grab the Zoloft and go into the living room and sit on the couch. The bird clock above the stereo hits three o'clock, and a blue jay calls. The thing is, it doesn't sound like a blue jay, raucous and piercing. It sounds more like a mourning dove, which is about the only other bird call, besides the jay, I can come close to identifying. I've often wondered if the clock is defective. At noon and midnight, what's supposed to be the house finch calls out. At eight P.M., when Tim and I were sitting down to dinner, we would hear the supposed cry of the black-capped chickadee. It was probably really the tufted titmouse, or the white-breasted nuthatch.

Maybe he'll come back for the clock. I'll stay home from work and surprise him in the act of taking it down off the wall, and we'll sort things out.

But probably he knows it's faulty, and that's why he left it. He'll get a new, completely different clock. It probably won't make a sound.

I think I'm feeling something now, and it doesn't feel bad. Valium. Why didn't I ever know about Valium? It's starting to take the edge off. First the edge was a solid black line in my brain, and now it is a quavery one, a loopy, swirly, black line, dissolving like stitches in a wound that's almost healed. No wonder Tim always wanted to go down to Mexico.

I get up, feeling floaty. At the end of the living room is the counter that divides it from the kitchen, and out the kitchen window is the Pacific Ocean. I love to watch the sunlight skittering over the water by day, and the fairy lights of the oil platforms at night. I never actually go down there, never take the elevator to the garage and walk out the metal door to the beach. But I have this bright idea, so I go down the hall and wait for the elevator and soon I am standing outside our building on a square of cement, at the edge of the sand, blinking in the glare.

The sand grains swarm my feet, over my sandals. I keep walking. I don't mind. I go down to the water and let the waves wash over my feet. When I was little, when we lived in Pompano Beach, Florida, I'd splash around in the Atlantic. But then my mother decided the salt water was too damaging to my hair. She yanked me out one day—I remember I was six, because I was still barely eligible for the Tiny category in the Little Beauties pageant—and after that I was only allowed to swim in pools, dog-paddling to keep my head above water. I still don't know how to swim properly.

Behind me somebody's radio is playing "You're Just Too Good to Be True." I imagine a man and woman embracing to kiss. They unstick their lotion-slick bellies and walk up the beach hand in hand, entering one of the apartment buildings. They shower together under cold needles of water, lathering soap all over each other. Their love is clean and good and true.

I open the plastic pill bottle and throw the cap at the waves. A big, dirty gull swoops down and scoops it up in its curved beak. I toss the pills at the ocean, and they disappear in the sudsy froth of a wave coming in. I wonder if the seagull will choke on the cap. So what. Serves it right. Let it plummet into the sea and get washed up on shore and have its dead eyes plucked out by other seagulls, it's not my problem. I hate the beach.

7.

I N the Before, everyone's a blue field of energy, part of the larger field but still distinct from everyone else. The Before feels weird to Stella. It's exciting, but very disorienting. They've all moved away from the Light, where they didn't have any shape at all and never thought about it. Everything just flowing through, no sense of where you ended and anything else began: that felt normal. Here there's a sound like dangling chimes. There's a buzzy hum under that, a nervousness about what's coming. Stella's here, but also in her mother; she drifts toward the other unborn, falls away, watches Jamie's life and sometimes the lives of the other mothers-to-be.

Right now it's all about the mothers. Of course, the babies have picked their fathers, they did the best they could with the available men, but at this stage the men are sort of secondary. Right now the unborn are all about the amniotic fluid, the nudging of the mother's internal organs, the tangly umbilical. Everyone's curled up and feeling cramped. Sometimes there's a father's hand or cheek laid on a mother's belly, and a little ripple passes through, like an oar disturbing the surface of a lake. But the mother's slightest mood change is a seventy-five-foot yacht churning through. When she's upset, or really unhappy, forget it. It's downright scary. Like being carried out on a riptide and smashed by a tsunami, then dragged over a coral reef.

What's happening now is terrifying. Stella feels the contraction as Jamie doubles over. Jamie gets up and staggers across the beach, and Stella's consciousness is slammed back and forth between the Before and her mother's belly. It's jostly inside Jamie, and it hurts. Each contraction makes Stella feel a kind of suffocated panic. She tries to focus on the waning sound of the chimes, not to look at the way the Before seems to be expanding and shrinking, then shredding all around her. Suddenly, getting born seems like a bad idea. The worst. What was she thinking? Her mother is a miserable depressive and doesn't want her. Jamie had seemed so sweet and lost when Stella was in the Light, watching her from afar. Stella had wanted to help her, to be with her. What happened to that feeling?

Stella's slammed back deeper into the Before, the blue field whole again, pulsing. She watches Jamie walk along Ocean Boulevard. Jamie stops every few minutes to moan, then falls to her knees under a jacaranda. She stays there while a few petals swirl down around her on the sidewalk.

"Ow, ow, ow," Jamie says.

Stella gets slammed back into Jamie's uterus. It's dark. Stella's whole body aches. She wants to scream.

8.

JAMIE weaves toward a gas station on the corner. She sat on the beach for a couple of hours while the contractions got more frequent. Her water broke and soaked her jeans. They're still wet. She has to call her mother. Her mother will say, "Oh, honey, thank God you called me," and tell her what to do. The gas station is only a row of pumps and a small building, a box inside of which sits an Indian man in a yellow turban, taking credit cards and money and dispensing cigarettes. There's no pay phone. She is supposed to have a cell phone, like everyone else.

A man is putting gas into a white Mercedes convertible. He stands leaning against the driver's side door, smoking a cigarette, his back to her. She crosses in front of the Indian man behind glass, steps to the cement island and grabs a few paper towels from the dispenser. She's sweating like crazy. She wipes her face and rubs at her jeans with the towels. There is no bathroom to go into so she can take off her jeans and hold them under the hot air of a hand dryer. There is never a bathroom when you need one. The world was designed for men, so they could spend their time drinking beer and high-fiving and punching each other in the stomach instead of doing the dirty work of life, like having babies. This is way worse than being punched. She makes it to the edge of the gas station driveway, and then another pain hits her. Are they supposed to come this fast, so soon? She can't remember. For a while, she went to childbirth classes given by her mother's midwife friend, sitting around a living room with a bunch of couples, but then she quit going. She refused to study for this baby. Now it is here, a week early, like a pop quiz.

"Hey. You need help?" The man with the Mercedes has pulled up beside her, looking up at her with what might be concern behind his mirrored sunglasses.

"Hospital," Jamie says, seeing her face magnified grotesquely in his glasses, her face swelled up like her pregnant belly. Soon she will be back to normal. She'll get a navel piercing, a steel ball on one end, an arrow point on the other. She'll be free.

"Get in." He leans over and pushes open the passenger door as she staggers around the front of the car. He is wearing a white T-shirt and white shorts. Two tennis rackets are on the floor of the passenger side, and he picks them up and tosses them in the back. As soon as Jamie falls into the car, he hits the gas and she is slammed against the tan leather seat.

"So, where is it?" he says.

"What?" Another shudder goes through her. It's like trying to withstand an earthquake. She's not one of those high-rises that's going to sway back and forth on its reinforced steel rods. She feels more like an old brick building, or a mud hut. She is going to implode. The car seems suddenly too confining; she turns and climbs halfway up the seat as the next contraction hits.

"Where's the hospital?" the man says. "I'm not from here."

"I don't know, exactly." Jamie tries to remember. She has only been there twice. When she was seven, she broke her arm falling out of a palm tree in a neighbor's yard. She was trying to reach the top of the tree to see what was up there, among the beautiful fronds. What was up there, at the very top of the tree, was a brown rat. It peered down at her, its whiskers twitching. She screamed and let go. All she remembers of the hospital that time is a set of glass doors, and a lady doctor who kept calling her Janey.

The second time, after her father's head injury, Jamie was kind of drunk. She sat in the car with her eyes closed while her mom drove. Her father was hooked up to machines, his head wrapped in bandages. Leaving, she tripped over a cord and fell against a chair. When she got home she went into the backyard to sneak a cigarette, but puked instead. For the rest of his stay she called him on the phone, drew him funny cards her mother took to him.

"It's sort of near the ocean," she says. She really has no idea.

He laughs. "Looks like we're in trouble."

"I'm sorry," Jamie says, thinking, No, we're not. You're driving a Mercedes, and you don't live here. You're not in trouble.

He puts his hand out. "I'm Anthony. Anthony Perillo."

He actually wants to shake her hand, like they have just met under normal circumstances. She stares at his hand, then lets out another moan. She feels like the cow she saw in a TV special. The cow was digging in its hooves as it was led to a man with a hammer, who was about to strike it dead between the eyes before turning it into hamburger, beef round, top sirloin.

"Don't you have a cell phone?" she says.

"Threw it away." He sounds happy about it. Jamie wonders if he is insane. Maybe he is a serial killer, cruising the greater L.A. area looking for pregnant girls to disembowel. Whatever he could do to her couldn't feel as bad as this does. Still, she hopes he's not going to try anything. Her mother would be so pissed to find out she had hitchhiked.

Another contraction. "I'm going to die," she says, when she can talk again.

"Me, too," he says. Still cheerful.

"Oh, shit, I forgot the teddy bear," she says, just realizing it.

"Look, there's a cop," Anthony says.

She looks. Several cars ahead of them is a motorcycle cop, stopped at the light, gunning his engine the way cops like to do. The light turns green and the cop takes off. Anthony roars after him.

9.

RULE #36: Do not reuse towels. This includes hand towels.

I WALK across the beach to the cement path and drop the empty pill bottle into a wire trash can. I stand there looking at the sand all around me, remembering a movie I saw once on the Sci Fi Channel, *Invaders from Mars.* It featured sand swirling around and sucking people underground. While they were underground, a mark was put on the back of their necks, showing they'd been taken over by Martians. A little boy was the hero. I fell asleep before I found out what happened to him, but I remember that sand. Now it shimmers on either side of me.

It's not like I'm really afraid of being swallowed by the beach. I am not crazy.

What I am, I see, is weak. I have just thrown my pills away.

No judgment, Sharon would say. Start again. Keep trying.

I want to rush right back to the safety of the apartment and wash off this sand. But I hear Sharon in my head, telling me that exposure is the key: confronting the contamination and not running from it. I feel very exposed right now. But also guilty about the pills. The Valium is helping the anxiety, a little, and I think maybe I should get with the program after all and take a walk down the beach. The sand is not going to kill me.

I turn and start walking south, away from my building, along the center of the path. It's not that wide, so when joggers come toward me I have to move over a little. I don't like jogging. It involves sweating, and going outside when you don't have to. Tim ran here early every morning. I am walking in his ghostly footprints right now, maybe picking up some of the molecules from his Nikes on my sandals.

Molecules get exchanged all the time, a continual, messy, back-and-forth commerce between you and the rest of the world.

Try not to think about it too much.

When Tim got back from his run, I'd usually still be in bed; I would hear him in the shower, and then I'd get up to take mine. While I showered he'd be making his breakfast in the kitchen, leaving me coffee he had poured into the thermos so it didn't sit cooking on the burner of the coffeemaker. By the time I got to the kitchen he'd have disappeared down the hall, into the room he used for his office. So it feels right to be trailing after him again, almost as if I'm going to catch up, finally.

A woman lopes toward me. She is a stick figure in a gray tankini, and thinner even than my mother. She makes me think of a starved greyhound chasing a mechanical rabbit down the track, like the races Gloria used to drag me to in Daytona Beach. After the woman passes, I realize I've seen her on a TV sitcom. It's funny how often I recognize people. Whenever Tim and I were in L.A., I would point out some ordinary-looking person who had been in some movie or on TV, in heavy makeup and different clothes, playing the sister of the murdered man or Flower Seller or Girl in Panty Raid. I could always spot them. The only people Tim ever recognized were Goldie Hawn and Kurt Russell, in a Starbucks in Santa Monica. Goldie Hawn looked young, except for her hands. Goldie and Kurt: one of the few Hollywood couples to survive.

I wonder if the path ends at some point, or if it goes all the way to Mexico. I will just stay on it, exposing myself to the salt air, the kicked-up particles of sand, the possibility of gull shit splattering in my hair. At the border there will be a big parking lot with all the cars lined up to cross, full of tourists and returning workers and smugglers, and then I'll turn around.

Or maybe I'll cross the border, walk along the shoulder of the road, and keep going. I will buy a large bottle of Valium, and swallow every single little blue pill, and then I will simply disappear. No more problems.

There is a sidewalk ahead, that connects the path to the street. Teddy's World is a few blocks down that street. Maybe I will never see Teddy's World again.

Another thin woman jogs by, outrunning the fat cells that are chasing her. Two girls on Rollerblades move spastically in my direction. I move to the right, to let them go, but then I see a Teddy's World teddy dangling from the taller girl's hand.

"Wait, stop!" I move back to the center of the path. "Where did you get that?"

The tall girl can't stop. She runs into me and grabs my arm with one hand to keep herself upright, her nails digging in.

"Hey!" her friend says, behind her. "Hey, what are you *doing*!"

I've taken a step back, but managed not to fall or bring the tall girl toppling over on top of me. I grab the teddy from her hand as she rights herself. It looks like the one I sold this morning. They all look alike to the untrained eye, but I know. I wind the key in its back and sure enough, "Für Elise" starts up.

"Give me that," the tall girl says. "It's mine."

"No, it isn't."

She yanks it from me, and I yank it back. I clutch it to my stomach. It's got sand all over it.

Good for you, I hear Sharon saying.

"What's your *problem,*" her friend says.

"Where did you get this?" I shake it at them, watching the sand fly off it. Little trails of blue sparks. I can't feel the Valium at all anymore.

"Nowhere," the tall girl says. "I found it. It's mine."

"Forget it, Christy," her friend says. "Let the bitch have it."

Christy looks down at me. If she were a man, she would realize two things: that she is bigger, and that it's two to one. If she were a man she would hit me in the face, take the teddy, and say, "Sorry, pal."

"Fine," Christy says, moving around me. "Keep the fucking thing."

Her friend clomps after her on the blades. "Whatever," she says.

"I thought this was going to be a fun day," Christy says. "All we've done is run into wacko bitches. Let's go to the mall."

"You always want to go to the mall," her friend says.

I stand there with the teddy. Maybe the pregnant girl who bought it walked into the ocean, drowning herself and her unwanted child. Maybe she just got bored with it really fast. She listened to "Für Elise" a few times and that was enough. Everything is disposable these days.

Sand crystals cling to the fur of its head and hands and feet. Sand is shining on its overalls, its red plaid shirt. Sand is crawling over my hands like millions of tiny ants.

Like I said, I am not crazy. Nobody likes to be covered with sand. Normal people get home from the beach and shower off the sea smell, the grit, the suntan oil. Normal people, after they use a public restroom, usually wash their hands, because there are all sorts of germs to watch out for. Pathogenic microorganisms. Bacteria, viruses, spreaders of disease. Germs aren't something I invented. This is what I told Tim, when he called me a nutball. I hate that word. I hate especially that he was right about my not being like normal people. When I use a public restroom, I usually don't wash right afterward, because I don't like to use the public sink. I rush home, my hands and arms itchy and burning, and shower for up to an hour. My hands are itching right now, either from the sand or from the memory of everything Tim said to me in our last fight, the day before he left.

"It's all about you, Diana," he said. "Your rules, your anxiety, your fucking mother. What about me?" he said.

There is only one thing that will help, even if it doesn't help for long. Soap and water, soap and water, soap and water. I need it in the worst way.

I drop the teddy on the path.

Diana, Sharon says in my head.

Okay, okay. I pick it up again. I hook one finger through its little blue-jean suspenders. Two lefts and I'm heading down another sidewalk, back toward the apartment. Maybe I will start collecting teddies—dirty, contaminated little teddies. They can keep me company in the apartment, now that Tim is not there, hunched over his computer. The computer is gone. It's one of the few things he took right away, one of the few things that mattered to him.

10.

STELLA curls her hands into fists. She wants to fight her way out into the world. No, she doesn't. She doesn't ever want to leave the Before. The world is a terrible place, filled with violence and stupidity and greed and cruelty. It is no place for an unprotected infant.

If only people could be born fully grown, and skip the help-less part, she thinks. Then she can't think anymore; she's turn-ing, she's upside down, being squeezed on all sides. Pulverized. She's a peach being squished by an enormous, cruel hand. Why didn't anyone tell her about this part? She had watched other babies disappearing from the Before, their blue energy sucked out. She had watched them emerge on the other end—pulled from their mothers and into the world—all of them wailing and looking like hell. Now she knows why. The Light is behind her somewhere, the wonderful, magical, streaming, marvelous Light. The Before is expanding and contracting all around her, blue shimmers turning black, pulsing blue, blue, hang on to the blue. Blue is good. Not as good as the Light, but better than any-thing out there in the black part, that round orb she seems to be getting closer to.

Wham. She's floating above the backseat of a car. There's Jamie, freaking out and screaming, a bunch of uniformed cops around her. A guy in shorts, with dark curly hair, is squeezing

Jamie's shoulder. He's talking to her quietly, the calmest one of the bunch. The cops are all saying "Go on, honey, push. It's okay. We're gonna get this little guy out." The cops look like kids at Christmas, like Jamie is about to deliver something they always wanted—a bike, a baseball glove, a fire truck.

Wham. The black orb has changed color. It's brightening. Not like the Light; this is a weak, watery brightness. A bad imitation. Stella's being pushed toward it. Her head is killing her. She can't breathe. What a concept, breathing. You have to depend on breathing, every instant of your life. You need oxygen, and food and water, and all the rest of it—you need a place to sleep, somebody to play with, somebody to love you enough to change your shitty diapers at the beginning and the end of things. Life is nothing but codependency. Stella sees it all in a flash, and then it's too late; her head is sticking out there into the air of the world, out of Jamie's stretched vagina. For a second she thinks she can reverse the pushing somehow and get back, if not to the Before then at least back inside Jamie, but then with a great rush the rest of her slides out, into a pair of hands, and she's being held around the waist and lifted up, smelling leather and blood. She can't see very well. She's close to a face, a face that is definitely not Jamie's, a round, big-nosed cop's face that is grinning ear to ear, smiling at her with dingy yellow teeth. This is it, Stella realizes, and starts screaming her head off.

11.

RULE #20: The bedroom is the sanctuary.

RULE #21: Shower before getting in/touching
the bed.

RULE #22: Sit on the edge of the bed and put
socks on before putting your feet on the bed
(to keep germs from floor off bed).

RULE #23: Clean anything you take to bed—
book, laptop, phone.

RULE #24: Don't go in the bedroom with the
ceiling fan on unless you're very clean.
It could blow dirt around.

THE thing about beauty is that even while you have it,
you feel like you're missing out on whatever it's supposed to do for you. I was a beautiful toddler, but all I knew was
that adults liked to stick their faces, smelling of mint and alcohol and shaving cream, close to mine. They liked to pinch my
cheek, which sometimes hurt, until I got older and learned the
trick of sticking my tongue sideways in my mouth, against the
inside of my cheek, so they couldn't get a good grip.

When I started school, I learned that everyone had a special talent: one girl could add two-digit numbers in her head. A boy crayoned wild horses, their manes and tails streaming, galloping over the big sheets of butcher paper set on easels around the first-grade classroom. My best friend could hold her breath and make the irises of her eyes jiggle.

My talent paled in comparison. I stood on a stage. I smiled, batting my false black lashes over my wide blue eyes. I shook my long honey-colored hair and sang "Over the Rainbow," or played the one song I had learned on the accordion. Then some adult set a tiara on my head and draped me with a sash, or handed me a goody bag and a Certificate of Participation. Then we got in the car—by then, Gloria had found a man to buy her one—and drove a long way home.

My mother made me understand that everything was subordinate to my beauty. It didn't matter if I could sing (I could, a little); it didn't matter if I was the only girl in my category who could spell "synergy." My skills were the bridesmaids at a wedding, meant to enhance the bride's image, never to upstage her.

The bride was friendly and confident, always finding the positive in life.

The bride cared deeply about other people, especially the Poor and Less Fortunate, and wanted to devote her life to helping everyone achieve their fullest potential—including herself, of course, because when you achieve your own potential, you naturally want to help other people.

The bride had that inner quality, that special realness about her that everyone immediately recognized. Even if she had to fake it sometimes.

I hated the bride.

At fifteen, I killed her. After Freddy's Ford Cowgirl, I quit. No more of my mother's starvation diets. No more glittery ensembles from Pageant Palace. I cut my hair short with my mother's fabric scissors. I dressed in baggy Levi's and oversized men's shirts, and refused to wear makeup, and slouched around with my eyes on the floor, sullen and unresponsive. I ate Big Macs and Whoppers and Chicken McNuggets, and Hershey's Kisses by the bag, and my face broke out like a normal teenager's. I killed the bride, and though a few years later she began to revive, she has never recovered her former glory. Now you'd say I was pretty, but not the kind of pretty men cross three lanes of traffic for in order to offer her a ride.

Not the kind that can keep a man from leaving.

I'm standing naked in front of the mirror in the master bathroom, trying to see what Tim would see. I haven't really looked at my body in a while. I knew I'd been gaining a little weight, especially this year because of the meds, but I hadn't wanted to look. I remember my mother, thin as a praying mantis on her continual diet of Scotch and vanilla yogurt, pointing to some other mother after a competition, a mountain of a woman dragging along her crying, defeated little girl.

"Would you get a load of her," my mother said. "Please, somebody turn down the volume on that ass."

My ass, I see, is cranked too high. It sounds like one of those souped-up cars that cruise along Second Street. My thighs, too. My thighs could shatter glass.

"Look at you," I say to myself. "No wonder he doesn't want you."

I have taken two more of Tim's Valium, trying to calm down, but I am not calm. I see now that I am disgusting. The only good thing about being inside of this body is that, if I avoid mirrors in the future, I will not have to look at it.

I tried not to memorize Tim's new number. I didn't want to think it was something I would have to remember for a long time. They were easy numbers, though. Bad numbers, but easy. I put on my blue terrycloth robe and go into the living room and dial them.

"Talk," he says, picking up the phone. Because of his Irish accent, it sounds more like "Tok." The way he says certain words makes me weak.

"You left your Valium," I say. "Whydidjoudothat?"

"How many did you take, Di?"

"You know me so well. I don't know anybody who knows me like you . . . do. You do."

"Diana," he says. "You're not going to do anything stupid, are you?"

"I already have. I got my hair cut."

"I'm sure it looks great."

"No, it's all wrong. I just want to kill myself." I don't think Tim, or any man, can fully appreciate the pain of a bad haircut.

"Should I be worried? Should I call 911?"

"Why haven't you called me? You haven't called me." Tim and I talked on the phone a few times after he left. Not exactly talked. I screamed and ranted, and he listened, or pretended to. Sharon told me to stop calling him. Write down everything you need to say, she told me, but don't send it to him. I wrote it all down, like she said. But what good is a letter you don't send? I mailed it last week.

"I thought we agreed," Tim says. "It wasn't going to help us break up."

"I don't want to help us break up."

I try to imagine Tim's new place, the apartment he's been living in without me, but I can't. I just see him sitting on a kitchen chair, in space, holding a phone to his ear.

"You agreed," I say. "With yourself. Not with me." I fall a little sideways, to the arm of the couch, cradling the phone between my ear and the solid, reassuring arm. "I know," I say. "I'm a nightmare."

"For fuck's sake," Tim says. "No, you're not." *For fock's sayke.*

Noh, ye're naht. I can't stand how much I love his voice. I love it more than his gray-green eyes, which I love considerably.

"Blah, blah, blah, blah, blah, blah, blah. Blah," I say. I learned it from Shirley MacLaine, in *Terms of Endearment,* a movie about a mother and daughter. The mother is overbearing, and the daughter dies of some disease, and meanwhile the mother gets involved with the astronaut next-door neighbor, played by Jack Nicholson. When the astronaut tells the mother he can't see her anymore, she goes, Blah, blah, blah, blah, blah, blah, blah. Blah.

"All the washing," Tim says. "We've had this conversation how many times now?"

"I was getting better. You know how much better I was."

"And those fucking rules. There's more to life than rules."

"I got fat. Why don't you just say it." I pull the belt to open my robe, looking at my rounded belly. "I got ugly."

"No. You're beautiful," Tim says. "You know you are."

"How beautiful? Scale of one to ten?"

There's silence on the other end.

The worst part of competitions was when you were lined up onstage in front of everyone while the runners-up and then the winner were announced. If you were chosen as a runner-up, you breathed a sigh of relief because, thank God, at least your name was called and you weren't going to walk off the stage a total loser. But the next thought in your head was that you'd gotten close, so very, very close, and you hadn't won. You might be second runner-up, and there was a first runner-up and there was the princess, and you weren't the princess. And at those times when you *were* the princess—after they'd named the first runner-up and you'd sweated it out, thinking that since your name hadn't been called yet it was either one or the other, total victory or humiliating defeat (because being a finalist is not good enough, Diana, it is simply not acceptable, you have to aim for the top, do you hear me? Smile, baby. Straighten your shoulders)—well, being the princess felt amazing. It felt like all the light in the world was meant for you, all the smiles on the faces of the adults and the tears of the other girls.

"You can use decimals," I say. "Like, 9.2."

"I'm not going to rate you," Tim says finally.

"Or 8.75," I say.

"Bloody hell. Stop it, Diana."

"Come over."

"Bad idea."

"Come over, anyway."

I wait, listening down the wire to where he sits, maybe thinking it over.

"I can't," he says.

"Sure you can. Walk out your door, get in your car, take the 101—"

"Look, you're going to be okay."

"Please come over," I say in my little-girl voice. I do a really good little girl. I have fooled telemarketers into asking if my mother is home. Tim is charmed by this voice.

"No," he says.

I cup one of my breasts and study it, trying to imagine Tim's mouth on my nipple, or just his head resting there while I play with his hair. The breast feels heavy, like it's filled with milk. I used to have small breasts. When I was really beautiful, I had none at all. I wore a blue cowboy hat, a blue dress with blue leather fringes at the wrists and a triangle of mesh at my midriff. I wore beige nylons and blue cowboy boots, and the number 27, a good number, and everything on me glittered and shone. My hair reached to my waist and I put one hand on my hip and thrust the other palm out toward the audience, and I sang, *Stop!*

in the name of love, before you break my heart, and I didn't have a clue what it meant until this exact moment.

"Baby," I say. "Please. I love you."

"I'll always be your friend," Tim says. "You know that, right?"

"Oh, go to hell." I click the Talk button, and he disappears; the kitchen chair recedes beyond the galaxy, to the edge of the universe, Tim's blond hair a light that is eaten by a black hole. I dial Gloria's number. It's almost two A.M. on the East Coast, but she won't mind me waking her. She will be thrilled. Her daughter, her precious baby girl, can't make it without her.

12.

JAMIE wonders why the hospital is so noisy at night, considering that all these sick people are trying to sleep. Nurses and orderlies go up and down the hall with their shoes squeaking. On the other side of the curtain, in the next bed, a woman is lightly snoring. A monitor beeps occasionally. Someone is revving a motorcycle in the parking lot. A nurse comes in just as Jamie's finally dropping off, and checks the catheter they stuck in her earlier. The doctor said Jamie could have gone home tonight, except that she hadn't peed since before the labor started. It had made her bladder swell up. Or something. The doctor had explained it to her, but she was hurting too much to pay attention. She couldn't pee on her own, she knew that much.

I should never have let them bring me here, Jamie thinks. I already had the baby in the fucking car, what did I need the hospital for? I should have left the baby right then, just given it to the cops and walked away. Crawled away. Lain down and bled to death.

Anthony had followed the motorcycle cop right into the parking lot of a police station, honking like crazy, and a bunch of cops had come out. They tugged off her jeans and underwear while Jamie swore at them. She bled all over Anthony's backseat. One cop delivered the baby and another cut the cord and they all stood around with goofy smiles on their faces, like she was the Virgin Mary and not a knocked-up teenager. They had brought her here and called her mother, and Anthony had hung around for a while to make sure she was okay.

Even though there's a tube in her draining her bladder, she still feels like she has to pee. Everything hurts down there. Her whatever-it's-called tore, and the doctor stitched it up. She wishes he had just sewn it completely closed. She is never going to let anything in there ever again.

The baby is in a crib right next to the bed. The baby is a girl, but has no name. Jamie thinks of her as an It. As in, It has been very quiet all evening, after screaming like crazy when It first came out. It is very fragile-looking. The cop who delivered It had tried to hand It to Jamie, but Jamie refused. In the cop's arms, It looked around vaguely, crying, and the cop rocked It until It fell asleep.

"You're going to be just fine," the nurse says. "The catheter will come out tomorrow, and then you can take your little girl home."

"It's being adopted," Jamie says.

"Oh, I didn't know," the nurse says.

Jamie's mother had found an agency. They were supposed to take the baby right away; that was the plan. Jamie was supposed to have had the baby in the hospital, and someone would call the agency lady so that she would be there for the birth. Jamie would still be high on drugs, not feeling anything, when the baby was whisked away. Now it's all fucked up. The baby is there, in the crib. The agency lady will come in the morning.

"Do you want to hold her?" the nurse says.

"What for? To feel worse about it than I already do?" Jamie starts crying. Her legs ache, her breasts are sore. She is never even going to even talk to a boy again.

"You're her mother," the nurse says.

The nurse is older, and Latina. Jamie can tell she believes in motherhood, in family, in Jesus nailed to a piece of wood in his underwear.

"You should at least say good-bye." The nurse is bending over the crib, lifting the baby. The baby makes little snorkeling sounds.

"I don't want to," Jamie says. "I just want to go to sleep."

The nurse sits on the edge of the bed. She lays the baby down beside Jamie. Jamie can feel the hot little body against hers, burning through the hospital gown. Why is it so hot? Maybe there is something wrong with it.

"Is it all right?" Jamie says.

"Just hold her," the nurse says. "Such a little beauty. Aren't you the most beautiful thing. You got here early, didn't you sweetheart?" She strokes the baby's back. "You're going to be fine," she tells it.

The baby's face is scrunched up, its eyes slitted in its tiny face. Jamie can see its face clearly. A parking lot light is shining right in her window, through a crack in the curtains. Why don't they keep the rooms darker, so people can sleep? The baby plucks at Jamie's hospital gown, feebly. Those hands can't be real, they are so small. Like the paws of a rat. Pluck, pluck. Love me, love me.

I love you, the baby says. *Don't leave me. I came here for a reason.*

"What?" Jamie says. "Her hands look weird," she tells the nurse.

"They're a little blue, from poor circulation. That's normal, honey."

The baby's lips are puffy—collagen lips. They look too big for her. Her nose looks slightly flat. She has a little white hospital cap on her head. Thank God, she looks nothing like Kevin. She looks, weirdly, like Jamie's dad since his accident. Her eyes are open now, dark and slightly crossed.

"She's cross-eyed," Jamie says. "Is that normal, too?"

"The eye muscles aren't quite developed. She's perfectly fine. Do you want to try to nurse her?"

Jamie thinks of a pig she saw on an elementary school field trip. There were goats to pet, and peacocks and roosters walking around. The pig was lying on its side in a separate pen. Several blind-looking piglets were squirming all over each other to get to her teats. It was sickening.

"Otherwise I'll need to pump your milk," the nurse says.

Pumping doesn't sound too appealing. The word makes Jamie think of Kevin. She had once heard him say to a friend about another girl, "I'd like to pump her till I'm dry," when he thought Jamie couldn't hear him. "Okay, I guess," she says. The nurse helps her scooch up on the pillows, shows her how to support the baby's head. The baby only takes a few seconds to figure it out. After a confused nuzzle or two she clamps her mouth right down on the nipple and sucks.

It feels amazing, nursing a baby. The ache in Jamie's left breast turns to blissful release. Her whole body feels it. It's actually sexy. Better than sex, because there's no boy involved. Kevin and other boys had sucked on her breasts, usually with one hand heading down into her pants. She had liked it, but it was nothing like this. If someone could package the way this felt, nobody would bother with drugs anymore. No wonder that pig had just lain there, its eyes closed, smiling.

One of the baby's slightly blue hands rests on Jamie's breast. The baby drinks steadily, in loud gulps. Her eyes close. After a while she stops nursing. She lies in Jamie's arms, asleep. Her little mouth, fallen away from the nipple, hangs open. She is a wrinkly, bluish creature with spindly arms and a head like a misshapen potato. The nurse might be right. She might be the most beautiful thing.

13.

RULE # 33: Shower immediately when you come home if you've used a public restroom—and spray Lysol on the car seats.

MY mother doesn't answer the phone. She doesn't have a machine, so the phone just rings. I can't believe she doesn't wake up. Even passed out drunk, she has always responded to a ringing phone. But it must be that she is, in fact, too passed out. She would never ignore me in my hour of need. Fred takes his hearing aid out at night, so I know he's not hearing anything.

In the morning, when we finally talk, she'll probably apologize for all the hysterical phone calls today. I doubt she'll remember exactly what she said. It will be her usual hangover guilt, her feeling she must have done something terrible. That feeling will go away. She'll have a little vodka-grapefruit for breakfast, along with her soft-boiled egg. She'll put on her black bathing suit with the mesh at the front that shows her cleavage, go down to the pool with sunscreen, another drink, and *Pageantry* magazine, which she still reads to follow the scene, and plan my comeback.

I let the phone ring while the clock—the white-breasted nuthatch, or maybe it is the American robin—announces that it's 11 P.M. in Long Beach. When it sings again at 11:30, I hang up.

The Valium is making me sleepy. I don't want to sleep. I want to stay up and scream at someone, like my mother. I miss her. I haven't seen her since Christmas. On Christmas night, Gloria and Tim got drunk together on Scotch and danced around her living room to some cranked-up Van Morrison Tim put on, while Fred slept and I rewashed all the dishes in her cupboards. Tim loves to drink. On the basis of this trait alone, my mother had immediately taken to him as soon as she met him, and although she didn't want me to move to California, we were married with her blessing. Tim likes my mother, too. There is not a man on earth my mother can't charm. Maybe, now that I am out of the way, she will invite Tim to visit without me, and she will try to seduce him. Did I mention that my mother is promiscuous, even at this age? Right now she is having an adulterous affair with a fiftysomething bartender at TGI Friday's. I don't want to know any of it, but she insists on telling me. They usually fall for her, offering to leave their wives and girlfriends, buying her jewelry she sells as soon as she has it appraised.

I consider calling Tim back. When he left, he did it with a letter, a letter that said he was afraid he wouldn't go through with it if he actually saw me. The letter informed me that he'd already rented a place. He had a phone already. He had furniture. Everything he needed, in other words.

I stagger up and head for the kitchen. Some food is what I need to keep me awake.

I set the table: plastic place mat, square napkin folded once, clean fork in the center of the napkin so it doesn't touch the mat. The place mat shows a map of the United States, with the state flowers and state birds in squares around the border. I set down a glass of filtered water on the East Coast, and imagine flattening Gloria in her condo. Like an earthquake or tornado, my water glass descends and collapses the ceiling above Gloria's side of the bed. Fred, next to her, will wake up untouched. When I was in high school, a tree fell in a storm and killed a girl driving with her little brother, and the brother didn't get a scratch. Disasters like this happen every day. People blame them on God, but maybe there is some other force at work. Maybe we have more power than we know. My mother would never know what hit her.

I open the freezer and consider. La Fiesta Spinach Enchiladas, Nancy's Quiche Lorraine, chicken Parmigiana with green beans and applesauce. I have three choices. Well, make that two choices. I bought the parmigiana before I heard about chickens. I already knew about the problems with beef, what with mad cow disease making the papers every other day, but I naively thought chicken was okay to eat until Marlene, who's a lacto-vegetarian, started telling me how they're raised. Growth hormones. Antibiotics. All of them trapped in cages, stressed out and shitting on each other, misery seeping through their cells and handed on to us. "Eat free-range, if you insist on eating chicken," Marlene said. But who knows what they get into, roaming around on their own? Chickens are stupid creatures. Like babies, they probably put anything they can find into their mouths. Beaks. Whatever.

When we were first married, Tim would sometimes bring home a whole chicken, dripping pink juice that would spill onto the cutting board where he sliced open the plastic bag the chicken came in. He would loosen the skin to put pats of butter underneath, and stick his hand inside the cavity to take out the organ meats. I ate the chicken, but the thought of the juice bothered me, chicken juice getting into the porous wood of the cutting board and through the score marks of the knife. And even though Tim would wash his hands after cooking it, I couldn't stand for him to touch me, later, in bed. I'd think of the interior of the chicken, the slime of it still on his hands, and even though he'd wash up again, for my sake, he knew that if we ate chicken for dinner he could forget about making love later.

The best food, I've discovered, is the kind that makes you forget about where it came from in the first place. After our first couple of years of married life, we pretty much left fresh food alone. Even canned food was suspect. Cans can rust, the beans or tuna can spoil. Food that was frozen, then microwaved— that's mostly what we ate. Tim didn't really mind, once he got used to it. That's what he said, anyway.

But I guess, after all, he minded. About the food, and about all the rest of it.

I toss the chicken parmigiana dinners, all five of them, into the trash, and turn back to the freezer. I take out a Nancy's quiche. It's the kind for one person, the mini-pie that lets you pretend you are not really getting just a tiny taste of things. I tear open the square cardboard box, and the quiche falls on the kitchen floor.

Face up, though.

Still, it's the floor.

I go for the sponge mop in the utility closet, open up a fresh sponge, and put it on the mop handle. I drag out the bucket and the 409 and fill the bucket with scalding water. I throw away the contaminated quiche, feeling a rush of hunger and frustration; now I'll have to wait for the floor to dry before I can start again.

There are several rules involving the floor, but that's not the worst of it. The worst is when I can't remember if I've followed a rule correctly. Take the laundry, for example. I might take the damp clothes from the washer very carefully, making sure they don't touch the edge of the washer since then they'd have to be done over. But once I get them in the dryer and close the dryer and am about to turn the knob to seventy minutes, I pause. Maybe the clothes *did* touch the edge of the washer, and I just didn't notice. I try to think back, to see the clothes coming out, to watch in my memory for a dangling sleeve or a stray sock. The truth is, I just can't be sure. So I have to take the clothes out of the dryer and put them back in the washer.

Sometimes this goes on for hours.

I leave the kitchen floor to dry and go down the hall, to the second bedroom that Tim used as his office. Tim's a freelance web designer. He can work anywhere. I look at the desk we bought together, an old-fashioned wooden desk, the kind with drawers on each side and one in the middle. They are hard to find now. Modern office furniture is cold and modular. What are called desks are really only tables, with interchangeable cabinets on rollers. If you leave your spouse, they are easier to move.

There are a few holes in the bookshelf, so Tim must have taken some books. I alphabetized them for him, and I dusted them regularly. Dust is piling up on them right now, and on Tim's collection of Day of the Dead figures. Little clay skeleton mariachis, skeleton pool players and dog walkers and weightlifters. Dead woman at a computer. Dead couple in a rowboat, a little red bottle of wine between them. Dead bride and groom, holding hands. They take up a whole shelf, and they are hell to dust because they are so fragile. Every year, more than forty million tons of dust settles over the United States. Dust from blowing soil, from volcanoes and forest fires, from cars and factories spewing tiny particles that get carried by the air. Even the ocean makes dust. The water evaporates in the spray, and leaves the chemical elements from the salt. I've looked it up; "Know your enemy" is my motto. I've never heard this, but I have a theory that some dust comes from the cells of dead people and animals, the way rain is made of water that seeps into the ground. Why else would the Bible say "Dust to dust"? Maybe the cells come up from underground and are drawn into the atmosphere, and then sift down little by little. With rags, with Dust-Off, with the vacuum attachment, I may be constantly encountering tiny pieces of dead matter. One thing I know for sure: There is no way to really get rid of dust. It's like nuclear waste, only worse. Even plutonium has a half-life and will decay, hundreds of thousands of years from now. Dust is eternal.

I sit in Tim's chair. Or on it. It's not really a chair; it's some weird-looking backless, slanted thing his chiropractor recommended. How can Tim be gone, when so many of his things are here—his plastic Magic 8 Ball, the coffee tin holding scissors and pens and a ruler, his seashell full of colored push pins, his black Swingline stapler, his wife? I pick up the Magic 8 Ball. I shake it and ask if Tim will be coming back.

In the black circle, the blue triangle floats up, the answer written there in white capitals: REPLY HAZY TRY AGAIN.

I bought him the Magic 8 Ball for his thirty-fourth birthday, in July. I bought him a case of Guinness and a bottle of eighteen-year-old Glenlivet, which I got at a discount from Liquor Barn, where I am still on very good terms with the owner. I bought him a black silk shirt, and I made him a chocolate cake, which I didn't eat but which he seemed to enjoy. He must have been apartment hunting already. After we made love that night, he must have been thinking he wouldn't be lying next to me, listening to the sound of the washing machine down the hall, for much longer.

I shake the Magic 8 Ball once more. I concentrate on imagining Tim walking in the door tomorrow afternoon, removing his Nikes, walking down the hall in his white socks. He sets his laptop on the desk. He is carrying roses, fresh from the Farmer's Market. He takes the scissors from his desk and goes to the kitchen and cuts the stems over the sink.

He sweeps up the stems with his hand, and drops them into the garbage. He puts the flowers in the black vase with some water and opens a little packet, pouring in the white granules that will make the roses last, and sets them on the hallway table so they'll be the first thing I see when I come home from work. Then he puts some frozen enchiladas in the oven for us. When I come home the house will smell like Mexico, like the Rosarito Beach Hotel where we used to stay, where waiters brought us margaritas by the pool and a line of horses was tethered on the beach. I will take a rose between my teeth, and dance into the kitchen with my arms raised above my head, snapping my fingers. Tim will put his hands on my waist. He'll twirl me in my stocking feet.

DON'T COUNT ON IT, the 8 Ball says.

14.

STELLA feels like she should be paying attention to everything: the tense conversations yesterday morning in the hospital, the car ride, her new surroundings. It's just that she keeps falling asleep. Focus, Stella thinks. This is life, this is important. Since yesterday they've been at her grandparents' house, the house Jamie grew up in. That voice on the couch is her grandmother. Grandma Mary. Stella remembers being in the Before, watching Grandma Mary talk and wave her hands around, wearing a dress with sleeves that fell away from her arms and revealed miles of bracelets. She must be wearing them now. Stella can hear them clanking. Everything is kind of blurry.

Jamie is holding her, and it's hard to concentrate on anything else. It's not the Light, or even the Before, but it's not bad. Mom has this thing called milk. It's bluish white and sweet, and it tastes amazing. Milk makes everything else secondary. All Stella wants is some more of it. And for Mom not to let go of her.

Okay, listen. Pay attention. This is life.

"This is not going to work," Grandma Mary says. "I can't take care of your father, and you, *and* a baby."

"I'm keeping her," Jamie says. "She's mine."

"This isn't like Buffy," Mary says.

Buffy. Who's Buffy? Stella wonders. And when does the milk

come back? She gazes toward Jamie's breast. It's in there some-where.

"I know, Mom," Jamie says. "I know she's not a goddamned dog."

"You went on and on about how you wanted a dog. Then we got Buffy, and what happened? You ignored her. You never fed her. I was the one who walked her, who took care of her."

"You loved that dog. You made it yours. You fed it ham-burger. That dog never liked me."

"We agreed that you were giving this baby up."

"I changed my mind. I didn't know it would feel like this. Look at her," Jamie says, holding Stella up. "Isn't she cute? She's adorable. I want her. She's mine."

It feels good to be raised into the air. Zoom. Then down to Mom. Mom's big face, the Cherry Chapstick smell of her mouth. The lovely milk smell. Mommamommamommamom-mamom.

"You didn't even care when Buffy died," Grandma Mary says.

"Just because you were a basket case," Jamie says, "doesn't mean I had to be." She bounces Stella a little. Bouncy bouncy bouncy. Stella feels her eyes jiggling in her head. Life is a roller-coaster ride. It's a big amusement park with rides that sling you around, with flashing lights and crazy music, cool air on your skin and pee and stuff coming out of you and hands that tickle your feet or count your fingers and toes. Life is a blast! Faces come close to yours and smile and talk in goofy voices like they're cartoon people, and you get all the milk you can handle. She never knew. No wonder everybody hung around waiting to get here. No one had told her.

"We're getting off the subject," Grandma Mary says. "I don't want to talk about Buffy."

"You brought it up."

"A child is not a dog."

"Duh, Mom," Jamie says.

"Don't you get sarcastic with me." Grandma Mary sounds angry.

Stella looks her way. No one told her about being half-blind. Is this what life looks like to everybody? She has to reconstruct the vision of Grandma Mary, out of what she remembers from the Before. Long hair in gray and black corkscrews. Big wooden parrot earrings poking out of her hair and swinging back. Stella squints and can make out a couple of spots of rainbow light, zipping back and forth, from sun coming through the crystals hanging in the living room window.

"I'm calling the agency," Grandma Mary says. "I'm calling them to send someone over here, and this time you are going to sign the papers."

The papers, Stella remembers, were a big deal at the hospital yesterday morning. The soft squishy woman had talked about the papers. She had held Stella for a couple of minutes. She had something small and square and shiny pinned to her jacket. The woman smelled funny. Stella shit her disposable diaper, and the woman handed her to someone else.

"I'm not signing them," Jamie says.

"Then you're not living under my roof," Grandma Mary says. "This is your karma, not mine. You deal with it. Take responsibility, for once in your life."

"That's not fair," Jamie says. "I don't have anyplace to go."

"Life isn't fair," Grandma Mary says. "Do you think it's fair, what happened to your father? He tries to make a decent life for himself. He works his butt off to get ahead. Then look what happens."

This is interesting. Grandpa. There is no sign of Grandpa yet. Something has happened to him, Stella doesn't know what. This ignorance is frustrating. From the Before she had watched

Grandpa on the couch, drooling in front of the TV, eating from a bowl of Chex Party Mix. Sometimes he knocked over the bowl and it would just sit there upside down on his lap or on the floor, until Grandma Mary came in and put it back on the table. He didn't look like he'd be that much fun, but maybe he would be nicer than this angry rainbow woman with the clanking bracelets.

"Don't blame me because of Dad," Jamie says.

"You are not keeping the baby," Grandma Mary says.

"You can't tell me what to do."

"As long as you are under my roof, I certainly can, young lady."

Grandma Mary starts yelling, and Stella tunes out. Mom will handle it. It's time for more milk, though. She feels a little bereft, a little cranky. A creeping feeling of desperation and loss overtakes her. This must be hunger. It has to be taken care of; this won't do at all. The rides are stopping. The carnival tents are sagging and collapsing, the pretty lights have all turned black.

Jamie has set her on the couch. Mom? Pick me up. I need some. *Now.*

That doesn't work, so Stella tries screaming the way she did when she first got here. Turns out that works like a charm.

15.

RULE #39: Shower after any contact with
an animal.

THERE'S a baby screaming inside the house. I stand on
the porch, waiting for the screaming to stop before I
knock. The porch is filled with plants, in plastic and ceramic
pots and redwood tubs. Objects hang from the ceiling: a purple
donkey piñata, a wooden duck painted bright blue, a satiny
crescent moon, cylindrical metal chimes, a shriveling spider
plant in a macramé sling.

"Call Gloria," I say into my cell phone.

Gloria's phone rings. No answer.

Sharon suggested I might want to limit contact with Gloria,
because of how she stresses me out. That maybe I shouldn't be
calling the east coast twice a day to talk to a woman who makes
me feel bad about myself. Sharon said I had enough stress in my
life, with Tim leaving and trying to deal with my OCD. For a
while I was doing really well. Setting boundaries. I called just
once every couple of days, and I hung up when Gloria was
drunk and became abusive. Now I haven't returned any of her
calls. She doesn't know I tried to reach her two nights ago, and
again last night. She probably thinks I hate her, and so she has
gone on a bender. Right now she is in an alcohol-induced coma
at Fairfax Hospital. Or she is sitting on a bar stool at TGI Fri-

day's, talking with her younger lover, having an aneuristic event and sliding in a heap to the floor. Or she is driving around drunk, weeping over her failure of a daughter. She loses control of her Cadillac and veers off the George Washington Parkway, crashes down the wooded slope, and ends up sinking into the Potomac.

The knocker on the door is a naked bronze angel. Angels are always depicted as females, I've noticed, even though I remember reading once that angels are supposed to be male. Lucifer was an angel. I wonder what he looked like. Probably nothing like the happy little winged girls in the mobiles we sell at Teddy's World, wearing white gowns threaded with gold, Valley Girl smiles on their faces. Lucifer probably had skulls tattooed all over him, their empty black sockets dripping blood, inky worms slithering down and turning into real worms, crawling over his big jackboots. The worms go in, the worms go out. The baby stops screaming, all of a sudden.

I lift the naked bronze angel by one wing, and she falls with a heavy thud against the door. Jamie Ramirez will be glad to get her teddy back. I kept it for nearly forty-eight hours. I sat it on the living room couch, sand and all. But I couldn't sleep that night, and yesterday when I got home from work I threw it in the washer a couple of times to decontaminate it. You can kind of tell—the fur looks a little bedraggled—but it still plays the song.

A woman opens the door, a woman who looks slightly deranged, an ex-hippie on a bad acid trip.

"Hello," I say, "Mrs. Ramirez?"

"Who wants to know?" she says, suspicious.

I wave the teddy at her, like it's identification. I am not a Jehovah's Witness, or a Sierra Club canvasser. I'm not going to tell you that you are damned to hell, or that Mother Earth is being murdered by her children. Don't be afraid, Mrs. Ramirez.

"Is Jamie here? She bought this the other day at my store."

This is the address Jamie Ramirez wrote on Marlene's mailing list. I guess she had her baby already. That was fast. Two days ago she was a girl walking around with a soccer ball for a stomach, and now she's got a kid. Life turns on a dime, Tim always said. He liked American expressions. He liked American noir films and American baseball and American music and American cars. Liked, liked, liked. I deliberately think of him in past tense, as though he's dead. It would be so much easier if he were dead. I'd have gotten a phone call, or a visit from a nice policeman. Some huge accident on the 101 or the 405, a hopped-up semi driver hitting a guard rail, the oil-filled tanker fishtailing across three lanes, a seventeen-car pileup. I'd watch it on the news that night, crying into one of Tim's shirts. Tim's Ford Explorer would be nothing but a hulk of charred metal. There wouldn't be any body to identify. He'd just have vanished, ascending into the smog layer.

"Your store," Mrs. Ramirez says. "What store is that?"

"Teddy's World," I say. "Everything for your baby and toddler needs."

Here's what I figured. I return the teddy this girl lost, and maybe she comes back into the store sometime. Or even if she doesn't, I casually mention to Marlene that I have gone above and beyond the call of duty. Marlene gives me a raise. I am named Employee of the Year.

And maybe I'll get a reward. People are always giving money to strangers who return things. They're grateful, they feel an obligation. Sometimes they are extremely generous, they are so happy to find an honest person.

A thin black cat jumps down from a wicker loveseat and slithers around my ankles. I give it a gentle nudge, but it comes back. Its front paws look like black-and-white baseball mitts with too many fingers. It is deformed in some way. There are probably fleas snuggled into its fur. The bubonic plague was carried by fleas, and it's still around. There was an outbreak in L.A. in 1924. Plague can lie dormant for years, traveling between fleas and mammals, before suddenly infecting humans. This could be the moment it decides to make its comeback. I kick at the cat again, a little harder. It looks up with a feral face. I can sense it is about to attack.

"She bought this for her baby, I guess. This is her home, right?"

Mrs. Ramirez still looks spooked. I smile reassuringly and glance down at her feet. Birkenstocks. I take a step back. Her toenails are about six inches long and painted metallic green. They look like the thin, elegant claws of an exotic animal it is against the law to own. I wonder if this house is under some evil spell, if everyone's feet are cursed, even the cat's. I look back into her eyes, to keep my mind off what's down there.

"This isn't a good time," she says. She stands there looking at me. She's a big woman with knives on her feet.

"For the baby. Is the baby all right?" I try to look past her, but all I can see is a hallway. Newspapers are piled against one wall. Where there are piled newspapers, there are more cats. I inch backward a little more, holding the teddy in front of me, praying she will just take the damned thing. The cat streaks in between her legs, leaving a faint blue trail.

"Oh, hell's bells," Mrs. Ramirez says. "Come on in. I'm sorry. It's just been a hard morning."

I don't want to go in there, where I will be trapped with Dagger Woman and dirty animals, listening to the bells of hell. "Just give this to her, please," I say.

"No, no, no," Dagger Woman says. Now she's had a complete change of heart. "Come in. Please. I forgot my manners entirely. It's just been so crazy." She opens the door wide and moves aside.

The house is evil. It is going to draw me inside it, and this witch is going to mumble strange words that will turn me into a flea-ridden cat. I have seen pictures of fleas up close. They are as hideous as you would imagine.

"I really don't want to bother you," I say.

From inside the house comes Jamie Ramirez's voice. "Mom? What's going on?"

"A woman is here," the witch says. "She says you bought a teddy bear at her store."

I close my eyes. I can do this.

"Can I use your bathroom?" I say, handing her the teddy.

"Of course, dear. This way."

She leads me down the hallway. There are no more piled newspapers. The walls are covered with paintings and framed etchings—more angels. Also fairies, and unicorns looking at their reflections in rivers or cavorting through fields. They're pretty good, if you like that kind of thing.

The bathroom turns out to be surprisingly nice. It's big and clean. Part of it is soil, rich black soil in a square set off from the rest of the bathroom by a low tiled wall, next to a wall of thick green glass bricks that let in the light. Healthy plants are growing there, green and fresh. It's the kind of nature I like, neat and confined. The rest of the bathroom is done in colorful tiles. Even the sink is tiled. I wash my hands three times. I want to live in this bathroom forever. Maybe I can grow vegetables in the soil. I'd have all I needed: food, a place to shower and bathe, even music if I brought the teddy in here with me. I could live with it, now that it's been decontaminated. I could crank it up and listen to "Für Elise" over and over.

After washing, I feel a bit better. I don't want to dry my hands on the towel, even though it looks clean, so I wipe them on my pants.

I head back down the hall, then turn into the living room. The living room, too, is nice. There's a big-screen TV, a couple of black couches, a marble-tiled floor. This woman's way into tile. Jamie is sitting on one of the couches, nursing her baby. The teddy's seated beside her. Dagger Woman is nowhere to be seen.

"Hey," Jamie says. "Is this really mine?"

The mutant cat is sitting in a corner of the room on a tall carpeted platform, holding either a toy or a dead rodent in its mouth. The tail dangles down.

"I found it on the beach," I say. "I'm pretty sure it's the one you bought."

"That is so cool," Jamie says. "Look at my baby," she says.

The baby has her face attached to Jamie's nipple. I can see the blue veins under the skin of Jamie's swollen breast, and the thinner veins in the baby's forehead.

"Beautiful," I say. "What's her name?"

"Tiffany," Jamie says. "Lorelei. Nikita. Arianna. Delilah. I don't know yet." She looks up at me. "My mom doesn't want me to keep her."

"I thought you were going to give her up for adoption."

"Nope," Jamie says. "Not anymore."

Her mother comes into the living room. She sort of sweeps in, like a diva.

"I'm Mary Wagner-Ramirez," she says. "So good of you to come by."

"Of course I had to," I say, "when I realized that the bear belonged to your daughter." A hundred dollars, I'm thinking, wouldn't be out of the question. I give her what I hope is a winning smile.

"I just had to check on your father," she says to Jamie.

"Dad likes the baby, I can tell," Jamie says.

"It's not about *liking* the baby," Mary Wagner-Ramirez says.

"Don't *you* like her?" Jamie says. "She's your granddaughter."

They're talking like I'm not even there. I look at Mary

Wagner-Ramirez's hands to see if they, too, have stilettos. They are normal hands, though. The nails are short, no polish.

"I'm glad I could return the bear," I interject. I revise downward from a hundred dollars to fifty.

"She's another being on the planet," Mary Wagner-Ramirez says. "She doesn't belong to anyone. The body is a gift we're given."

A lousy twenty dollars is the least they could do for dragging me across town like this.

"Well, she was given to me," Jamie says. She shifts the baby. The sound of sucking fills the room. Gulp, gulp, gulp. The baby clutches at Jamie's shirt with one hand and waves the other one erratically in the air.

"We can't afford to keep her," Jamie's mother says. "All our money went into buying this house."

"Our old house was fine. We can move back there, I don't care."

Okay, fine. I'm not getting anything from these people. Another minute, to be polite, and I can go. I sit on the edge of the other couch, as far away from the cat as I can get.

"We're not moving," her mother says. She turns to me. "I'm sorry," she says. "My husband is disabled. He's a contractor. He got hit on the head with a hammer, by one of his workers. Twice."

"He was attacked?"

"Oh, no, it was a friend," she says. "Accident. Anyway, we just bought this house last year."

"It's lovely," I say.

The sucking sounds don't stop. The cat is batting around whatever dead thing it has found. When it's done, it will come for me.

"I have to go now." I get up and practically run for the door. I can hear the cat clawing its way down the carpet thingie.

"I have to get back to work," I say. "It's my lunch hour." I have to try to reach Gloria again. I imagine her opening her mouth to say my name, calling to me from beneath the rushing waters of the Potomac.

"Thank you so much," Jamie says behind me.

"You're not keeping it," her mother says.

16.

JAMIE drags her suitcase off her bed. It's a big green suitcase and she has overpacked it, as usual. Her mother always lectured her about packing light for family vacations, but Jamie always took too much. Too much according to her mother, but not according to Jamie. She needs her clothes with her. She will have to come back for the rest.

The baby is tucked into an armchair, wrapped in a Mexican blanket, sound asleep. Milk coma. She takes up hardly any room. She's like a doll, only better. Her eyes aren't plastic. One day soon, when her eyes uncross, when she can see really well, she will look at Jamie with total love. None of Jamie's friends have babies, not even Leila. Those girls are just girls. Jamie is a mother. Her tits have gotten huge, too big for a bra. In the tiny T-shirts she likes to wear, her tits look obscene.

Jamie has a lot of great clothes. She bought them in used-clothing stores all over the greater L.A. area. She bought some on eBay. Leila gave her some cool, more expensive things when she was tired of them. Jamie's closet pole sags under the weight of hanging blouses and dresses jammed tightly together. Her dresser drawers are permanently open, clothes exploding from them. The floor of her room is a sea of shirts and pants and dresses and handbags and shoes and underwear and hats and scarves and belts and socks. Every couple of weeks, when she got bored with what she had, she would fill a grocery bag with clothes and take it downtown to Mania, trade in what she could for store credit, and come home with more. It drove her mom crazy.

"Who are you?" her mom would say. "What do you need all these clothes for? I raised you to be a feminist."

"Chill, I just went shopping," Jamie said.

Her mom would go off on some rant about narcissism and objectification. Now Jamie won't have to listen to her anymore. She is taking her baby and leaving. She will have to hitchhike, but so what.

Right after Diana left, Jamie's mom had gone off to her studio in a huff and cranked up the New Age music. Jamie can hear whale songs drifting across the backyard. Her mom's studio is a big wooden shed in the yard. It has two stained-glass church windows that she found somewhere, that Jamie's father installed before his accident. In the studio, there is an eight-foot-high wooden statue of St. Nicholas, draped with rosary beads. St. Nicholas, the patron saint of children. Her mom had told Jamie all about St. Nicholas. Some children were kidnapped by an evil butcher, or fell into a well, and then, thanks to St. Nicholas, they were miraculously returned to their grieving parents. Her mom is in there making an etching of winged sprites hovering over a toadstool, or something just as stupid. Jamie hates her mom's art, though she used to love it, when she was little and didn't know any better.

The suitcase is on wheels, and has a pull-up handle. It's not so bad to maneuver on flat ground, but it's too heavy to drag down the stairs. Jamie lays it on its side and lets it go. It sleds down the dozen stairs and hits the tiled floor at the bottom with a loud whump.

"Whoo!" her father says from the living room. Her father used to play handball on Sundays, and drive his Chevy pickup to and from work, and make pizzas sometimes using Boboli crusts her mom would buy. He used to sit with her and play speed Scrabble, which was more fun than regular Scrabble. They would turn over one letter at a time, and whoever could make a word would call it out first and assemble the word in front of them. You could steal each other's words back if a letter was turned over that would make a new word out of your opponent's. Her dad was really good at doing that. He could see a word like "REAL" in front of Jamie, and then an "N" would come up and he'd immediately rearrange the letters in his head and call out "LEARN," and steal Jamie's word. He used to beat her all the time. He used to talk in complete sentences, too.

"Whoo!" her father says again. "Pilot." There is no telling what he is talking about. Jamie hopes her mother didn't hear the suitcase crash down.

She goes to get the baby. Leila bought Jamie a BabyBjörn carrier when she first got pregnant. As a joke. "Ha ha, very funny," Jamie said. She hung it on a hook in the back of her closet and forgot about it. Lucky it's there, or she would have had to carry the baby in her arms, and take only a backpack of clothing. She pulls the carrier from the hook. It's blue denim. She has put on a shocking pink tank top, for contrast. The baby doesn't even wake up when she lifts her and settles her down into it, slipping her little arms and legs into the holes.

Jamie looks at herself in the full-length mirror on the back of her bedroom door. Important and formerly important phone numbers are written there in bronze lipstick. Girls from high school. Boys she met at the mall or downtown. The number at Kevin's house, where Kevin's room is probably occupied now by a boy as cute and stupid as him, screwing some girl who will pretend to orgasm. Leila's dorm at NYU, and her new cell phone number. Jamie finds a pen and writes both numbers on the heel of her left hand. She puts on more lipstick, rolls glitter onto her bare shoulders. Her stomach is kind of big, but the baby and carrier hide it pretty well.

"Luna," she says to the mirror. "Nina. Anna. Cleopatra."

She used to have this trouble naming her Barbies. She would change their names all the time. They had stupid, little-girl names: Na-Na. Princess Leia. Ariel.

"Who are you?" Jamie says softly.

The whales swim back and forth in her mother's studio, singing. Whales can sing to each other through miles of ocean. There is some sort of tunnel or something under the water. Jamie saw it on the Discovery Channel.

She goes downstairs to the living room. Her father is singing, too, sort of.

"Yah, yah, yah," he sings. Her mom has dressed him today. His chest is broad, his arms are big and muscular and deeply tanned. His mouth hangs open.

She kisses him on his forehead. "'Bye, Dad," she says. "I love you."

"Yah, yah, yah," he says.

17.

RULE #8: Take care that water doesn't splash up from the sink when you're washing your hands.

"TEDDY'S World, where babies are our business," I say. On the other end of the phone, somebody breathes hard, *huh-huh-huh*. I can't tell if it's a man or woman.

Tim, I think. He is outside, on his cell phone. He will be walking through the door any minute, shoving aside that fat woman coming in with her stroller. He'll carry me out in his arms. It will be like Richard Gere coming for Debra Winger in *An Officer and a Gentleman*. All the customers in the store will clap. Marlene and Kelly will have tears in their eyes. "Way to go, Diana," Kelly will say. Tim will drive us home and put his Nikes where they belong.

Whoever it is hangs up.

Marlene thought up the slogan about our business being babies. I think it's a little cold, but for some of our customers it fits. These women went down to Mexico or South America, or over to China or Romania or Kazakhstan, and bought their babies. Some women are desperate to have kids. There is something wrong with these women, if you ask me. They get to a certain age—my age, usually—and all their regressive programming kicks in. They have to be mothers, no matter what. If they can't have a baby, they will just go out and buy one. If they are lesbians, they head for the frozen sperm.

Tim wanted children. Now he can have them, with a woman who believes in them. He'll have no problem meeting someone. A cute guy like Tim, who has a good job, who wants children. He probably already has women calling him day and night, women who can sense an available man. They drop by Teddy's World just to stroke the tiny sundresses and miniature leather jackets and imagine the children they'll produce to fill them.

I feel sorry for Jamie Ramirez. She almost escaped the baby fixation. Two days ago, she didn't want her baby. Between then and today, something happened, like in *Invasion of the Body Snatchers*. She fell asleep, and woke up a pod person, wanting her baby, wanting to be like everyone else. Probably, if she gave up this baby for adoption, she'd still end up shopping for another one when she turned thirty-five.

Here comes the woman with the stroller. She might look hugely pregnant, to the untrained eye, but I can see that she is only fat. She is a large mother who will never lose the extra pounds her baby added. I smile at her. I have taken more Valium. Teddy's World is not so bad. It is infinitely better than the rest of the outside world. The clothes are on the racks, sorted by size. The stuffed lions live with the other lions on their shelf, the dolphins live with the seals. The seals have zippers down their bellies, and their pups are tucked away safely inside. I live behind the counter right now, with a box of fragrance-free Huggies Natural Care Baby Wipes. We don't sell them, just keep a box behind the counter for customers to use in case of baby elimination emergencies. Lately I've started using them to keep the phone clean, and for my hands, between ringing up purchases.

"My husband said this is a good store," the woman says. "I don't know why he said that. I can't find what I need."

"What is it you need?" I say. A new wardrobe, I'm thinking, looking her over. A good liquid foundation for your face. Haircut, highlights, nose job, orthodonture, facelift, tummy tuck. You need your stomach stapled when you heal from the liposuction.

"A SnugRide car seat," she says.

"They recalled those in March," I tell her. "There was some hardware missing on some of them, so they couldn't be securely attached to the base. They were dangerous."

"Well, when are they making them again?"

"I don't know. Just think, if you'd bought one of those and gotten into an accident, it could have been awful."

"That's the one my husband says is good," she says, pushing the stroller back and forth with one hand, kind of fast. She's probably trying to give her kid whiplash. She probably wants a faulty car seat.

"Say you had the windows open and were hit broadside. That baby and car seat might fly right out the window."

"I thought he said SnugRide," she says. "Maybe it was SnugSeat. Does that ring a bell?"

"Or say the window was closed. Wham, right against the glass. Maybe the door would have been unlocked and flown open, due to the impact."

"Snug Something, he said."

I can't believe this woman has a husband. How could anyone love her? Maybe he doesn't love her. Maybe they married young, like Tim and me, and he loved her then, when she was just a little overweight, before her face and the rest of her went south. Maybe he got used to her being there, over the years. Then one day he woke up and took a good look at her, and wanted out. But by then they had a kid. He was stuck. He couldn't leave her. He went to the bar and had seven beers and threw some darts, hating his life.

Maybe, if I'd had a baby, Tim wouldn't have left.

"My husband—" she says. It's a tic some women have, beginning every sentence that way. *My husband says. My children need. My yoga instructor tells me.* These women have no selves. They've managed to completely disappear.

I understand, in a way.

She picks up a CD-ROM from the rack on the counter. *Baby Cha Cha Gold.* It's a bunch of clips of the animated baby who made it big a few years back on *Ally McBeal.* Marlene didn't think it would sell, but it does really well as a gag gift for showers. It outsells *Poker Babies.* It's got dancing baby, drunk baby, doggie doo baby, beheaded baby. Shakin' ass baby, old baby, cliff fall baby, bye-bye baby. She reads the back for a minute and puts it down.

"Blood all over the street," I say. "That tender little skull slammed against the unforgiving pavement."

She finally tunes in to what I'm saying. "For God's sake," she says. "What's wrong with you?"

"Everything," I say.

"Get help," she says, and turns on her heavy heel. She lumbers toward the door. The stroller is tiny compared to her, the baby in it even tinier. Poor little thing.

"Have a nice day," I call out, for Marlene's benefit. She's back in the crib section. "Thank you for visiting Teddy's World," I say. "Think of us for all your baby and toddler needs," I say, though she's already left. The Huggies wipes are all gone. I take a box of Tushie's Wipes out of my leather backpack. Unscented, with aloe vera and vitamin E. "We care about your baby," it says on the box.

I try Gloria's number again. I've been calling her all day. She is lying in the bathroom of her condo on the beige rug, choking on her vomit, and Fred in his vibrating lounger cannot hear her. She has gone swimming in the pool and hit her head against the wall, and the lifeguard is too busy flirting with some girl to notice her floating, face down, in the shallow end. The phone just rings. I go through seven Tushie's Wipes listening to it.

18.

JAMIE walks down the sidewalk, rolling her suitcase behind her. It's a warm, sunny day in Long Beach. It usually is. Sometimes it's a mild sunny day, or a cool, hazy day. But mostly it's the warm sun, day after stupid day. Today she doesn't mind. Today she has a whole new life; the old one is gone forever. She's not walking to the bus stop to go to her stupid high school, or to work at the stupid mall, or over to Kevin's to lie underneath him like a dead person and then smoke pot and watch a stupid video. She's not walking around pregnant and hating herself, feeling trapped by the thing growing in her stomach, hanging around the stores downtown to get away from her dad's drooling and her mom's incense. Everything is different now. She won't be eighteen for three more weeks, but she is already a woman. This is what her mom can't get through her stupid head.

Her mom will be upset to find her gone. Jamie left her a note: *I love you, Mom, but I love my baby too. I hope you will understand one day. I will let you know where I am after I turn 18. Love, your daughter and your grandaughter.* Jamie had put a sunburst around "grandaughter" with a red pencil, wondering if there was another "d" in it. Consonants have always given her trouble. Words like roommate, necessary, embarrassment—she always puts in too many letters, or too few. Eventually her mom will have to come around. In the meantime, Jamie hopes she doesn't call the cops.

It's a beautiful sunny Saturday. People are out doing things to their flowers, washing their cars, walking their dogs. They are her neighbors, but she doesn't know any of them. They look at her and she smiles and says hello. The old Jamie never talked to strangers. She hunched her shoulders and ducked her head, letting her hair swing across her face. Now she gives her hair a little toss and looks right at them. They are the ones who look away, after taking in the baby, the suitcase, the five-inch platform sandals she's wearing.

After a couple of blocks she has to rest. She's still pretty sore down there. In the adrenaline rush of packing and walking out, she hadn't realized she was quite this sore. Shit. She parks her suitcase on a street corner, in the grass under a tree, and sits on it. The baby—Melissa, Maya, Mika—is still sleeping. Jamie bends her face to the top of the baby's head, to the thin swirl of dark hair. She takes deep breaths of baby smell.

All of a sudden, she can't get up. Her stomach is cramping. She's tired and hot. Maybe she will go tomorrow. She doesn't really know where she's going, anyway. She has forty-two dollars, and a hundred and twenty more she can get from the bank. It's probably not enough for a plane ticket to New York. And Leila lives in the dorms. Leila has a roommate, a girl she doesn't like, named Darla. Darla will take one look at Jamie and the baby, and report them to the R.A. R.A.'s, Leila explained, are Resident Assistants, slightly older students who make sure the dorm rules are being followed. Even at college, away from your parents, there are people to act like your parents.

Maybe her mom will come looking for her. Jamie can go home and start again tomorrow. She can crawl into bed like she did yesterday and her mom will make her Yogi Tea, which is Jamie's favorite. She can watch TV all day again, with her baby curled beside her. *Blind Date* will be on. *Ricki Lake.* Endless reruns of *Mr. Ed* and *Bewitched* and *Buffy the Vampire Slayer.*

Her mom was wrong; Jamie did love that dog. It wasn't her fault it got hit by a truck. Buffy had run out the door, when Jamie opened it, and straight into the street. It was supposed to be Jamie's dog. She had named it, but her mom had stolen it. Her mom fed it from the dinner table and took it into her studio while she did her etchings. Buffy slept right on her parents' bed, near her mom's feet. When her mom ran errands, she took Buffy with her. Jamie never had a chance with that dog.

The baby stirs in the carrier. She wakes up and looks around vaguely, then in the direction of Jamie's face. For a minute she is quiet, gazing up. Then she looks worried. She twitches and draws up her legs, her face contorting. Jamie touches her bottom through the carrier. She can't tell if the baby has pooped or not; the disposable diaper works really well. It could probably stop Kryptonite rays. In another instant she can smell it. The baby turns her face back and forth, making small sounds.

"It's okay," Jamie says. "Shh. Don't be fussy."

The baby doesn't understand. If she understood, she wouldn't start crying like that. For such a new little creature, she got the crying thing down in a hurry. It's loud, too.

"Stop," Jamie says. "Stop it." She is sweating. She hurts all over. She looks down the street, but there's no sign of her fucking stupid mom.

19.

RULE #15: Clean laundry can be folded on the bed only. If it's set anywhere else, it can't be put away in the dresser.

I'M going to lunch," Marlene says. "Hold the fort."

"I'll keep the savages at bay," I say.

Marlene laughs. She thinks I'm the funniest thing. It almost makes me like her sometimes.

"Kelly has a doctor's appointment, so it's just you." She says "doctor's appointment" disapprovingly. No employee of Marlene's is supposed to require a doctor's care during store hours, or to need to leave early for any reason; I'm the only exception. I get special dispensation, because I work my ass off and stay late for no pay. Since starting in May, I have not taken one sick day. I have computerized the entire store, made the billing system more efficient, and found cheaper suppliers for no fewer than eleven baby products. I have never been late. I come in on Sundays to do the inventory for the week. I've left early exactly twice—the day after Tim left, and yesterday. Marlene hasn't said a word about it. She just told me to work on Monday, which is usually one of my days off, and I said no problem.

"If I'm not back, just close up, okay, sweetie?"

"Of course. If I don't see you, have a great rest of the weekend." Marlene likes taking off for lunches and not coming back.

She goes with a woman friend or two, spends the afternoon getting plastered on appletinis at L'Opera, or Balzac's in Belmont Shore. They eat dinner, and then return to the bar area, trying to meet men. Sometimes she comes back to the store before dinner, drunk off her ass, and I take her in the back and settle her on a bean bag chair and she sleeps it off there. I'm used to taking care of drunks. I used to drag my mother in off the lawn in front of our apartment building all the time. I'd come home from going to the movies with a friend, or someone would drop me off after a party, and she'd be curled up between the sidewalk and a row of bushes. I'd wake her up and she'd climb on piggyback, and I'd hunch forward and carry her the few yards to our door. She wasn't heavy. Marlene, I think, can sense this history. She feels secure with me. She leaves the whole store, which usually requires three people to run it, in my hands, on a busy Saturday.

I call Gloria as soon as Marlene is out the door.

"Hello," she says, sounding sleepy.

"Gloria," I say. "Where have you been? What happened? Are you all right?"

She laughs. "I'm fine. Fred and I went to Annapolis for a couple of days. We had nice dinners at a restaurant on the water, and stayed at a lovely little bed-and-breakfast."

"I was worried."

"Don 't worry about me. What about you?"

"I don't know."

I've never told Gloria about the obsessions, the rituals. I don't even remember when they started; it seems like they were always there, like I was always having to pay attention to things. I remember being about five, in the car with her, holding my breath and feeling like I couldn't let it out until I saw seven red cars go by. I was always doing things like that, and I always felt like I had to hide it, like it was something private and somehow shameful. When I was first in pageants, I would count to nine, over and over, waiting for my turn. If my name got called on one or three or nine, it was bad luck. There were good numbers and bad numbers. The numbers thing mostly went away by the time I was twelve or thirteen. Gloria never realized. I don't think she realized about the washing, either—that started in my senior year of high school. She used to yell at me for taking long showers, and buy me Jergens lotion for my dry hands, but I don't think she knew what was really going on. How can I tell Gloria that I see contamination everywhere, that trying to keep myself free of it has taken over my life? She's disappointed enough in me already. Plus, she doesn't believe in psychiatrists or therapists. It's a racket, she says. Feel bad? Have a cocktail. Smile, and the world smiles with you.

"I talked to Tim," I say. "I couldn't help it. I called him."

"And?"

"I don't know."

"You're so indecisive," she says.

"Gloria," I say, "I feel so bad. I don't know what to do."

"There it is again. Stop saying 'I don't know.' Do something."

"Like what?"

"Where are you working now?"

"You know where I work."

"You change jobs so fast," she says, "I thought this week it might be something else. Why don't you go on some auditions?"

"Because I don't want to be an actress. Because I'm too old."

"You're not too old." The word "old" bothers her, like the word "mother." Even as a child, I had to call her Gloria.

"I am. For Hollywood, I am."

"With that defeatist attitude," she says, "no wonder you're unhappy. No wonder—"

"Don't say it."

I am supposed to hang up now. But I just stand there behind the counter, pulling out Tushie's Wipes one after another, while Gloria says, "No wonder he left. If you'd only try a little harder. How much do you weigh now, honey? You know you have a problem with that. Men don't like flabby women. Or depressed women, either. Do you know why men like me? Because I'm *fun*. Because I *enjoy* life."

Thank God the store is busy. Two people come up to the counter at once, and a third is trying to get my attention over by the strollers.

"I have to go," I say.

"Talk to you tomorrow, honey," Gloria says.

I ring up a Jumbo Music Ball and some GoMobile Farm Animals with Stacking Rings. Then I go and talk up the Clean Shopper, which is made of washable material and fits over the nasty seat in the grocery cart to keep the baby from teething on the disgusting cart handle. Babies have ended up in the emergency room because of that. Then I just stay behind the counter and watch people shop, and ring up whatever they buy. Ball Party Bounce. Cool Tools Box. Puppy Love Play Set. No one's buying anything serious. They want everything gift wrapped; everyone is headed to a fun birthday party, this afternoon or tomorrow, and everyone is buying fun toys and games.

Marlene is off drinking and laughing it up with her friends.

Soon it will be Saturday night. Date night, party night. All hell will break loose. Total strangers will exchange bodily fluids. Somewhere, blood will be spilled, ambulance and police sirens will wail, and I will be alone with a frozen dinner, safe in my apartment, safe and completely alone all night.

20.

LIFE is a series of reversals, Stella thinks. Got to get used to that. Mom seems to stress easily. All that yelling at Grandma Mary. Grandma Mary was pretty stressed out herself. Stella's glad they left Grandma Mary's house. She felt secure in the carrier, up against Mom's chest. But then, just a little walk down the street and Mom was sitting there crying. Stella's own crying had set her off. Or maybe Mom had pooped her pants, too. Things were looking pretty bad, but then a man in a big car stopped and gave them a ride. There was cool air in the car, a delicious chill on Stella's skin. There was some kind of thumping music that went right through her, and she just rode the vibration until the man dropped them off.

Now they are in the best place Stella has seen yet. Not that she can see so well. It's all a blur of bright colors. But she recognizes it as the store where Jamie bought her the teddy bear. Stella had looked through the blue haze of the Before and seen the smiling faces of clowns and animals, the fish and planets and pigs twirling from the ceiling, the balloons and teddy bears painted on the walls. A little train chugs around up there; she can hear the whistle that sounds every time it rounds the turn above the doorway in back. Stella is in a fresh diaper, strapped into a seat that rocks back and forth. Not bad.

Her seat is on the counter of the store. Mom is talking to the woman behind the counter, rapidly rocking the seat with one hand. Still stressed. What's the problem now? Life is fine again. There goes the train whistle. Stella knows the children on it are waving. She tries to wave back. The right arm jerks up a little bit, not very high. And her hand won't do that right-to-left thing. It goes in a little circle. Nothing to worry about, though. She'll get it.

"My mom says I have to give her up," Jamie says.

"She seemed pretty upset," Diana says. "Maybe she'll come around, though."

Diana is the voice behind and above Stella's head. Diana is the beautiful goddess of the store world. Stella hopes Diana will let them live here for Stella's time on earth.

"Right now she's just so freaked out about my dad and everything," Jamie says. "It's too much for her."

Rock me, Mom, Stella thinks. Jamie has taken her hand off the seat in order to bite her nails.

Another woman sticks her face near Stella's. "Ooh, da baby!" she says. "Wookit da little teeny baby!"

"I can ring that up for you," Diana says.

"So cute!" the woman says.

"She's mine," Jamie says.

"That's my granddaughter," Diana says. "This is my daughter, Jamie."

Jamie laughs. "Yeah," she says. "Mom."

"Oh! Well." This woman's vocabulary is terrible, Stella thinks. She seems too old not to know more words.

"Have 'em young," Diana says. "That's what I say."

Stella tries to squirm around in her seat to see Diana's face. She can barely move, though. Babyhood is kind of confining, so far. When does the walking part come, and the part where she gets to sit on the beach with a plastic bucket and shovel? She wants to dig, she wants to smack the shovel on wet sand, she wants to splash. And what's this about Diana being Jamie's mom—does that make her Grandma Diana? What about Grandma Mary? Maybe this is her other grandmother. She never got a look at her dad's parents. She remembers her dad. Kevin somebody. He was handsome, with dark hair that stuck up. He made a pyramid of Budweiser cans that took up one wall of his room. He lay on top of Mom, then rolled over and lit a joint.

"Well, well," the woman says. "Hey, wittle baby!" she says.

Maybe she is retarded, Stella thinks.

The woman is trying to put a rattle in Stella's hand. Stella's arm jerks and knocks it to the floor. "Oopsie woopsie!" the woman says. "Wittle baby dwopped her wattle!"

Jamie picks it up for her and sticks it in the seat beside Stella. "Here ya go, kid," she says.

The retarded woman goes away with whatever she bought. Is that what happens here? People come and take everything away? Stella hopes not. The store world is full of so many amazing things. What if someone takes the train? She listens anxiously. It's still up there. Good.

"Don't you want to clean that first?" Diana says.

"Uh, I guess so," Jamie says, and takes the rattle away.

"Ahh ahh unh," Stella says. She knows the words, but they won't come out.

"I'll just go and wash it for you," Diana says. "Be right back."

"Thank you," Jamie says. "You rock."

Rock. Good idea. Stella tries to throw her weight back and forth, but can't manage it. She sighs. *Come on, Mom. Rock me, rock me.*

"Shh," Jamie says. She pushes the seat back and forth. She puts the teddy bear next to Stella and turns the key in its back. "Here's your teddy bear," she says. "Laura. Alma. What am I going to call you? Who are you, kid?"

In the Light, Stella remembers, there was music. Or a feeling like music. Or was it that in the Before, she had the memory of something like music? She knows this song. When she was inside of Jamie already, soon to come out, Jamie had played it. She tries to remember more. Rock rock rock. It's hard to stay awake, hard to remember what the Light was really like.

"Elise," Jamie says. "Elissa. Lissa. Ella. Stella."

21.

RULE #25: Always keep the bedroom door shut.

I WASH the rattle in the bathroom and bring it out to Jamie
Ramirez and her baby, shaking it fast to get the water off
it. There are all kinds of things in tap water. Nitrates, chlo-
ramines, fluorides, calcium. Tiny microorganisms. Pesticides,
lead, copper, aluminum, chlorine. These are facts. I did not in-
vent contamination. The world is a toxic place; just ask the en-
vironmentalists. I learned a few things when I worked for Save
the Earth. Everything is connected, a great web of connections
through which the contamination travels. All I'm trying to do is
stay out of it. All I want to do is avoid that spider, coming out
of its crevasse in the earth to bundle me up in its sticky threads
until I'm suffocated, until it carries me down into its dark burrow and devours me.

I hand Jamie the rattle and stand on her side of the counter
while she puts it next to her baby. The baby is too young for a
rattle. It is too young to do anything but lie there. The baby
looks like all the rest of them. On the rattle is a picture of a
clown with a big red smile; it looks like all the rest of them, too,
like a baby sucking on a pacifier with a red shield. That's one to
be added to *Baby Cha Cha Gold*: dancing clown baby. I imagine
Jamie's baby magically slipping her restraining strap and run-

ning around on the countertop doing pratfalls. The baby gives
a little shudder, like she knows what I'm thinking: Babies are
ridiculous. Human beings are ridiculous.

"What's her name?" I say. I take one of her bare feet and wig-
gle it back and forth. It looks clean enough. She can't walk yet.
This foot has never touched the ground. I marvel at the notion.

"Stella?" Jamie says, like she doesn't know her own baby's
name.

"That means 'star,'" I say.

"Really?"

"Yeah, really." I can't believe people can get out of high
school and not know these things. "Like 'interstellar,'" I say.

"My mom would like that. She's big on the stars. Horoscopes
and shit. Constellations, motions of the planets, cosmic energy.
That kind of stuff."

"Spare me."

"Exactly," Jamie says. "That was pretty funny, saying she
was your granddaughter."

"That woman bought it. Stupid cow."

"Hah!" Jamie says. "You're so mean."

"I hate people," I say.

"So do I."

"My husband left me forty-eight days ago," I say. I didn't
mean to tell her that. It just comes out, probably because of the
Valium.

"What an asshole," Jamie says. "How could anybody leave
you? You're beautiful. You're funny. You're cool."

"I'm not beautiful," I say, wanting to cry. A little sob comes
up and I choke it back. One thing I've noticed about Valium: it
makes you happy, but also weepy. It sets you on that tightrope,
and you could fall either way. Below you are the clowns, the animals dressed up to look equally ridiculous, the restless crowd.

Below you, where the safety net is supposed to be, the spider is weaving away.

"Yes, you are. I love your hair. It's eighties Meg Ryan hair, all tously and adorable. You have amazing eyes. You could be a movie star."

"I used to win pageants." My eyes get wet and I wipe them with the back of my hand before any tears can fall.

"I'm not surprised."

"I hated it, though. I mean, I loved it and hated it."

"Yeah, I know," Jamie says. She strokes my shoulder through my blouse, a little circular motion. It's very soothing. Tim would just clap me on the shoulder, or the back, or slap my leg a few times. Easy, girl. Take it easy. Good girl.

"At least in a pageant," I say, "certain things were clear. You had a number. You had a routine."

"Yeah, but what's so great about routine?" Jamie says.

"You wouldn't understand," I say. "You think it's all a big adventure."

"No," she says. "I think it all sucks."

"What about your baby?"

"She's the best thing so far," Jamie says. "I want to keep her."

"Good luck with that," I say. "I mean it." I look at the baby. Her eyes are closed. It's hard to believe something so tiny and still could ruin someone's life.

"Hey, you live alone now, right? Since your husband left?"

I know where this is going. "Yes, but," I say.

"It must be lonely."

"It's not so bad."

"Liar," she says.

"I guess you're right," I say. "It all sucks. It stinks." I think of something I read at Fairfax Community College in a contemporary American poetry class. We read a lot of poems I didn't understand, and the professor talked about things like semiotics and the transcendental signified and refusal of closure. There was one poem I got, though. The opening went like this: It stinks. It stinks and it stinks and it stinks and it stinks.

"Most people don't get that," Jamie says. "They're all, like, 'Let's be shiny happy people, everything's fine.' It's like they refuse to see how fucked up the world really is."

Maybe this girl, in spite of her limited vocabulary, isn't so dumb.

"Maybe we could help each other," Jamie says.

"I don't think so."

"I'll cook for you," she says. "I'll clean. We won't be any trouble. Just until I can get my shit together. Or until my mom lets me come home with the baby. Please, Diana. Please please please. You're so cool."

"I can't." I have never been cool. When I was younger, I passed as one of the cool people, in school; because of my looks, the cool girls invited me to parties and sleepovers. But I knew I wasn't like them. I have always been the weird one, trying to pass, succeeding brilliantly.

"Wash your car. Your toilet. Do the shopping. Anything you want. All I need's a place to stay."

"I like it really clean," I tell her. "I have kind of a thing about it."

"I swear if you help us out you won't regret it," Jamie says. "You're a good person, I can tell. You returned my teddy bear. You didn't have to do that, you could have just thrown it away."

"I don't want a roommate." I look at her big green suitcase bulging next to the counter. It is larger than she is. It is full of clothing that will require washing. I look at her baby and see dirty diapers, drool and spit-up everywhere, pacifiers and teething rings strewn over the floor. I see Teddy's World as it might look after an earthquake, the shelves toppled, lions consorting with seals, OshKosh overalls in tangled heaps. The train has jumped its track and smashed into the carpet, killing everyone on board.

The baby twitches in her sleep, making the rattle fall again.

"Don't think of me like a roommate," Jamie says.

"What, then?"

"Just pretend I'm the maid," she says.

part two

PART TWO

22.

JAMIE wheels Stella down Second Street in a stroller with an awning. A quilted diaper bag attaches to the back. A little star mobile hangs inside the stroller. Diana brought a few things home from Teddy's World.

"I'll pay you back soon as I can," Jamie said.

"Don't worry about it," Diana said. "Tim's still paying the credit card bill."

Stella, at twenty-three days, is already building a decent wardrobe. She has booties and a bonnet and two sleepers and a nightie. She has a knit cap and lacy socks. Jamie can't wait to buy her more stuff, as soon as she has the money. Today Stella is wearing a teeny T-shirt with a rainbow on it, pink sweatpants, and rainbow socks. A striped flannel blankie is in there with her, just in case she needs it. At Diana's, Stella has a bassinet. When she's bigger, Diana will bring home a crib.

Jamie hasn't told her mom where she is yet. She called and left messages on the machine a couple of mornings, when she knew her mom would be at her Pilates class, just to say things were fine. Things aren't exactly fine, but at least she has a place, for now. She's got Diana's husband's old office for a bedroom. She's got a futon mattress that was already in there, and a new dresser to hold what she brought in her suitcase, courtesy of his credit card.

She's got Diana's rules, stuck in the mirror above the dresser.

Not that she exactly follows them. When Diana handed her the list on the first night—a list that started out neatly printed but toward the bottom got kind of scrawly, with crossouts and additions and little stars and exclamation points—Jamie nodded while Diana apologized.

"I know there are a lot," Diana said. "I'm sorry. Some of them just pertain to me, though. You only have to worry about the common areas. The kitchen, especially. That's the most dangerous room in the house."

"No problem," Jamie said. "I'll be careful."

"You can't just clean," Diana said. "You have to disinfect."

"Of course," Jamie said.

"It's best to let the disinfectant stay on the surface a while," Diana said. "Don't just spray and wipe. Let it sit there at least five minutes."

"I always, always do that," Jamie said. She jiggled Stella against her shoulder. Diana would be gone at work during the days, she figured, and what she didn't know wouldn't hurt her.

That's pretty much how it has worked out. Before Diana gets home, Jamie always clears the living room of all Stella's stuff. Diana doesn't know the floor's been covered with baby items all day. She comes in the door, looks around anxiously, then goes to change her clothes in the master bedroom, where Jamie is not to go under any circumstances. Like I would, Jamie thinks. Like I want to enter her precious inner sanctum.

Jamie stops the stroller and checks to see if Stella's fallen asleep yet. She's sick of walking up and down Second Street. Second Street gets old, fast.

Knocked out. Finally.

Jamie loves her daughter most when she's asleep.

Stella sleeps a lot, but not for long stretches. She's fussy when she wakes up, sometimes even after Jamie has given her so much milk you'd think the kid would explode. At night, there's nothing to do but walk around and around the room, carrying her. In the morning, when Jamie is exhausted and wants to sleep until at least noon, Stella's cries of hunger drag her out of bed. At least during the day, Jamie can take her out in the stroller. Then Stella shuts up and gets fascinated, looking around at everything or just gazing up at the stars in the mobile. The motion of the stroller eventually overcomes her, and she conks out again.

"Oh, the little darling," an old woman says, approaching them.

The woman is tiny and hunchbacked, her gray hair in a net. She is wearing a pink sweatsuit, the exact same color as Stella's pants. It weirds Jamie out, so she grabs the stroller and gets moving again. Once she's past the old bag she slows down and turns the corner. She stops in front of Mania, eyes a pair of jeans in the window, worn by a headless gold mannequin, and wheels Stella in.

Mania is the coolest place. Jamie remembers when she and Leila discovered it, right when it first opened. They had looked at each other and screamed. They had gone through the store snatching shirts and dresses and jackets from racks, spent two hours trying on stuff, and staggered out with heavy bags. Leila's bags were heavier, but that was okay. Leila tired of clothes quickly, and she was Jamie's size.

At Mania the floors are black rubber. Metal steps lead to a metal balcony. Everywhere there are clothes, clothes, clothes, clothes. Mania is a church, a temple, a holy shrine. Music throbs into Jamie's ears, a wave to ride as she cruises a circular rack of tank tops. All over the store there are mannequins in leather skirts and vinyl pants and see-through blouses and Mardi Gras beads. Girls slide hangers expertly along the racks, making split-second decisions about what they want to try on. Jimi Hendrix and Kurt Cobain and Janis Joplin and Bob Marley and Tupac Shakur are on huge posters on the walls. Even though they are dead, they are still cool.

The most expensive clothes are on the mannequins, or hanging high on the walls, too high to reach without getting someone to take them down with a pole. Jamie has a twenty-four-dollar store credit from a couple of months ago, which she hopes will be enough. She really can't spare anything from her diminishing cash. But she needs a new dress. Today is her eighteenth birthday. Diana found a babysitter for Stella, and tonight she and Jamie are going out. Diana's treat—she is probably putting it on the credit card, too—or they couldn't go anywhere. The money thing is getting to be a problem.

Fuck that, Jamie thinks, it's my birthday. Not a day to worry about that shit. Today I'm really a grown-up.

Plus, I can't wait to get away from this baby for a night.

The aisles at Mania are kind of narrow for a stroller. Jamie parks Stella over by the stairs. She has to shop fast. If Stella wakes up and is fussy, it's back to walking around.

There's a tank top she'd like to get, but she forces herself to leave it alone. She has to focus. She has to find the perfect dress, the one that will make her sexy and mature and irresistible. In the fancy restaurant they are going to, everyone will look at her and wonder who she is. Because of the dress she will have that special aura, the one that says, I Am Somebody. An actress in independent films. Or the star of her own music video. Maybe a cast member from *The Real World*.

Because of the dress, a boy will want to kiss her.

She's definitely not ready for anything else. Just picturing a penis makes her cringe. Even a soft penis. Maybe years from now, she'll be ready to let one inside her again. Maybe when she's thirty. Or forty. When Stella is grown.

But kissing would be nice. A boy's mouth, soft and open, his thick tongue lolling on top of hers. Downy hairs on his upper lip, or scratchy stubble, or smooth peach-fuzz skin. Boy breath: toothpaste and smoke. Her palms pressed against a boy's chest, feeling his muscles through his shirt.

God, she misses it.

Also, she misses going out. Hanging on the beach with the kids that gather there, or hitting a movie where she used to work. One of the ticket takers, a geek who has a crush on her, always lets her in free. This baby thing is intense. Diana gives Stella presents, and makes goofy faces at her, but Diana won't take care of her. Diana says she's not good with babies. Diana's a little tweaky, for sure. No help there.

It's the twenty-four-hour *Jamie and Stella Show*.

There's a whole rack of black dresses. Black dresses with zippers, with mesh or lace, with empire bodices and long flared sleeves or little spaghetti straps that cross in the back. Finally Jamie finds the one.

"Oh. My. God," she says softly.

It's a Betsey Johnson made of silk charmeuse, with a few small beaded flowers on it. It would probably be three hundred dollars, new, and here it is for thirty-eight dollars. Someone has to have priced it wrong. Jamie grabs it from the rack and looks it over, sure there must be something wrong with it, but all she finds is a tiny tear under one armhole, a seam she can easily fix. Size four. Can she wear a four? Her stomach's still kind of big. Well, she'll find out. She goes to get Stella. There's a line for the dressing rooms. The other girls in line don't even look at Jamie. Everyone acts cool, staring into space. Jamie does the same. When her turn comes, she pushes the stroller in through the plastic curtain. There's barely room for both of them. Wedged in, she whips her shirt off. She'll be able to tell if the dress fits without taking off her jeans.

From the dressing room mirror it's like another girl looks

back at Jamie, somebody mysterious and sultry and more curvy than Jamie's ever been. She has great cleavage now. The dress is a little tight over her belly, but she decides it looks hot. She digs into her purse and puts on eye shadow and some more lipstick. Now she can have any boy she wants.

"Stella," Jamie says, "your mom is a babe."

Stella has woken up. She's being good, not fussing. She gnaws on one fist, drooling, lost in her own world. One day Jamie will teach her about shopping, about how to find cheap vintage and designer clothing. One day Stella will be interested in what makes her look too short or too fat, what flattens her ass or pushes up her tits. Jamie will teach her about all that, and about the use of hair ties and facial scrubs and nonclumping mascara. Jamie pulls the dress carefully over her head, puts her shirt back on, and wheels Stella out. She uses her store credit and then lays out the rest in cash.

I'll come back tomorrow and sell my Frankie B jeans, she thinks. I'll get my clothes from home and go through them. I'll get my computer and set it up at Diana's and sell stuff on eBay, like I did last summer. I can make a couple hundred dollars, at least.

"Hey," the girl behind the counter says. "You had your baby."

"Yeah," Jamie says, flattered that the girl remembers her. The girl is a little older than Jamie, with black-lined eyes and black-and-purple hair piled on her head, a complicated hair sculpture made of tiny braids and sections that are held in clips and barrettes. She has tiger stripes tattooed up and down her bare arms, rings on every finger, and a T-shirt that says "Fuck the Earth." Jamie's been coming in here for the entire year this girl has been working here, but the girl has never acknowledged her. Usually she just takes the money and slides the plastic bag with whatever Jamie's bought across the counter, a bored, faraway look in her eyes.

in this universe. It's all getting kind of confusing. But this is the babysitter, Karen. Got it. Long Beach State sweatshirt, kind of spicy perfume, glasses to grab at: the babysitter. Check. This thing Karen is shoving at Stella's face is a bottle of formula. Okay, okay. She'll try it. Why not.

It's sweeter than milk. Not too bad, actually. Mom has gone out with Diana for a night on the town, because it's Mom's birthday. Jamie was born, too. It's hard for Stella to wrap her mind around that: Jamie as a surge of blue energy in the Before, waiting just like Stella to come down. The universes are so mysterious. Stella wishes she could go back. Maybe Mom could come, too. Where's Mom, again? She had it a second ago.

This formula stuff gives her a rush. Like the milk rush, only more intense.

"There you go," Karen says. "Such a good baby."

Stella sucks at the formula. In the Before, she could pretty much go wherever Jamie went. She wants to go with her, now. She wants to fly up and expand her field of vision beyond this face with the frizzy hair and glasses. To see Jamie in her beautiful black dress, out on the town with Diana. Diana, who as it turns out isn't her grandmother after all, but who seems nice, anyway. She keeps to herself a lot. Never actually holds Stella or anything, but that's okay. Stella only wants Jamie to hold her. She closes her eyes and wills herself to go to her. Get out of this body and just go.

"Rock-a-bye, baby, in the treetop," Karen sings.

In the treetop, over the trees, above the curve of the earth. Descending toward a planet with swirls of clouds around it. Down past all the lights, then the blackness of the Pacific. Low along the whitecaps. Coming in on a wave, a gaseous explosion of light; suddenly there.

"Did you come?" Kevin said. He flicked on a Tensor lamp set

on a wooden box next to the bed, and scrounged among the magazines and matchbooks, looking for his horn pipe and baggie of pot.

"Yeah," Jamie lied. "Couldn't you tell?"

Stella hovered right over them, flipped upside down and floated inside Jamie, flipped and hovered again. She felt Jamie's sadness as Jamie lay there with Kevin's come dribbling out of her. Jamie didn't know it, but one of his sperm had made it to the egg and broken through. The other sperm were like Kevin, slow and not all that interested. They trickled down her thighs.

Conception was a rush. Stella's soul felt flooded: with the room, with Jamie, even with Kevin at that moment. She was both of them and herself, too, and she was also still part of the Before. The Light was somewhere behind all that, rippling through her. Excitement, fear, energy.

Hi.

"You're kind of quiet," Kevin said. "Most girls, like, squeal and stuff. But I think that's when they're faking it." He lit the pipe with a Bic. The flame was yellow and blue. Stella was hypnotized by the sight of it. She moved up close to get its small warmth. She floated over the flame and tried to look in her father's eyes, but he closed them as he inhaled on the pipe.

"Want some?" he said.

"No," Jamie said. She was so sad. Stella was going to change all that.

Karen's still singing, "Cradle and all."

Stella wants to fly. The body she's trapped in won't let her.

24.

HOMEWORK: Confront the situations that
cause you distress.

S HARING makes me puke," Jamie says at the restaurant.
"I am so glad to hear that," I say.

We're at Balzac's, on Marlene's recommendation. Pink and
orange sunset colors, wicker chairs, water sheeting down one
wall, lit by candles. It's pretty soothing, if you don't think about
what might be going on in the kitchen. *E. coli,* fecal streptococ-
cus, salmonella. Mice and roaches. Food sitting out of the refrigerator, workers without hairnets, with cuts on their hands.

"Like, Siamese twins?" Jamie says. "That is so totally gross.
If I were a Siamese twin I'd want to kill myself. Or maybe kill
my twin. But then—" She stops, and I can see her imagining
how she'd do it. "I guess then I'd be dragging around this dead
twinlike *thing.* Attached to my head or wherever." She laughs
and reaches for her red wine. This is her second glass and she's
getting kind of tipsy already, I can tell.

The women at the next table are grazing off each other's
plates. They're a lesbian couple: a thin, stylish older woman
with white-blond hair, and a younger, darker woman who
needs to turn down the volume on her ass a few decibels. They
don't look like they belong together, but who knows. The older
one looks my way after she feeds a forkful of her entrée to her

girlfriend, and smiles. Maybe she thinks Jamie and I are also lesbians, or maybe she and her partner recognize me from Teddy's World. Maybe they have a thawed sperm baby at home right now, sleeping in a crib I have sold them.

"My mother had one rule," Jamie says. "Share everything. She used to live in some kind of religious commune. A bunch of them got together, made up their own church, and rented a house in San Diego."

"I think rules are important," I say.

"Your rules?" Jamie says. "They're a little intense."

"I know. I've been working on that." I made a list of the homework Sharon has given me over the past few months, and put it up on the refrigerator, next to the rules. I am doing my homework right now. Dining out is definitely up there in terms of stressful situations to confront. I look down, confronting the little dish of olives and bay leaves on the table.

Tim didn't like eating in restaurants, either. He used to work in one.

I once read about a little girl who died after eating watermelon from the salad bar at a Sizzler; the watermelon had gotten splattered with juice from contaminated sirloin.

Everyone knows this kind of thing happens, but most people ignore it, and eat out anyway. Just like most people, if they order veal, don't think about the poor calf living in its own shit, in a stall too small to turn around in. When they eat bacon for breakfast, or have a ham sandwich, they don't think about pigs being electrically stunned and then getting their throats slit, sometimes when the poor animals aren't quite out cold. Denial is the key to happiness. If you think too long about all the terrible things happening in the world, you will just want to kill yourself. Better to ignore the front page of the paper and flip straight to the Lively Arts section. Go to the movies. To the ball game. Buy an entertainment center. Fall in love.

The older lesbian at the next table keeps looking at Jamie. I can see why. Jamie put her hair up, and a few long strands curl down to her shoulders. Her neck is long and slender, her dark eyes are large and slightly almond-shaped. Her pupils catch the light from the wall sconces. She could have been a contender. If I were a pageant judge, I'd give her high marks on Natural Facial Beauty, Poise, and Fashion. I wonder if she has any talents besides getting pregnant and cleaning. She's very good at cleaning. Thank God.

"This is so awesome of you, to take me out like this," Jamie says.

"No problem. You've been such a help." She has, too. She does the grocery shopping. She wipes the doorknobs and mops the kitchen. She's there when I get home from Teddy's World, sprawled on her end of the couch in front of the TV, asking about my day. There is not one item of baby clothing on the living room rug, no trace of a stray pacifier. The baby is always in Jamie's lap, or tucked away in Jamie's room.

Jamie glances over at the next table, then leans in toward me. "Do you ever wish you could be like them?" she whispers. "It would be so much easier."

"I wish," I say.

"Then we'd be, like, perfectly content every night. Just hanging out and watching movies together." Jamie leans back and gives the blonde a smile.

Tim and I used to rent movies on weekends, but with Jamie it's a seven-night-a-week thing. I microwave popcorn. She usually picks the movies. At the end of almost every one there's a song that plays over the credits. Like in *Stepmom,* with Julia Roberts and Susan Sarandon, it's "Ain't No Mountain High Enough." When the song comes on, we get up and dance around the room. If the baby's up, Jamie dances holding her baby.

The thing is, though, I sometimes think about how she lived

with that diseased cat. And then she came into Teddy's World, where the contamination has already started. And nearly every day, I bring something home from Teddy's World.

I tell myself I can conquer this. I go to work, I bring home presents. I face my fear that I am polluting the apartment beyond the point of no return. I am not letting my fears rule me; I am staying and fighting. I am Employee of the Month again for September.

And I'm having more fun than I remember having with Tim for a long time. The movies Tim liked were in black and white. People shot each other, betrayed each other, lied and cheated and gambled their way to ruin. The movies ended with stern voice-overs explaining the moral of the story, or violins and cymbal crashes. They ended with Tim going to the kitchen for raspberry sorbet, and me going into the bathroom to shower before bed. Tim would stay up watching a talk show or the late news, and I'd usually fall asleep before he got into bed.

"No men," Jamie says, raising her glass and then finishing it. She gives me a goofy, buzzed smile.

"Exactly," I say.

"Can I have some more wine?"

"Sure." I look around for the waiter. Jamie can have anything she wants; it's her birthday, and Tim's paying for it. It's only fair that he cover the credit card bill, since I am now paying the rent on the apartment. I'm going to have to move soon, though, unless I get a roommate who can afford to help out.

"Let's drink to that," I say, raising my bottled water. "No men."

"No men," Jamie says.

The apartment, thanks to Jamie, is very clean. Tim's office has been transformed into a nursery, a little Teddy's World away from home. I told Jamie it all has to stay in that one room as much as possible. I made a few new rules for her, governing the Teddy's World items, the baby items, and the baby itself.

I called Tim to get the rest of his stuff, and he cleared it all out while I was at Teddy's World one day. 'Cos I'm movin' on up. I am woman. I will survive. Fuck Tim, anyway. Fuck men.

Our salads arrive, brought by the good-looking young waiter. He's somewhere between Jamie's age and mine. A tiny cross dangles from his left ear.

"Ladies," he says, and departs.

"More wine, please," I call after him.

"Too bad we're straight," Jamie says, watching him go.

I should be talking to Sharon about all this, instead of canceling our appointments and ignoring her phone calls. She'd be proud of me, for staying at Teddy's World and letting a stranger live in the apartment. She'd be proud of me for posting my homework on the fridge and trying to follow it instead of huddling in my bedroom every night with the Handi Wiped TV remote, proud to see me sitting in a restaurant eating salad just like any other normal, pathetically heartbroken woman.

"Too bad we can't live without them," Jamie says.

25.

IN the bathroom of the Lava Lounge, Jamie unpeels her dress down to her waist, unhooks her bra, and leans over a giant martini glass set on the toilet lid. Her breasts are killing her. She kneads one, and then the other, expressing enough milk from each of them to get some relief. Too bad Stella can't be here. Too bad Jamie can't nurse her in the bathroom, then hand her off to somebody before she goes back out to the bar.

Some of the milk misses, but she gets a full glass.

"So he was hitting on me?" a girl in the bathroom says. "And he wouldn't stop? So I go, Fuck off. Then he gets really abusive and nasty. Then he goes around telling everybody we were together. Which is a total lie. I would not ever be with that guy. Like, what planet is he from."

"I'm so horny," her friend says. "Let's go find some boyfriends."

"Just for tonight," the first girl says.

"Fuck 'em and forget 'em," her friend says.

Jamie fastens her bra and pulls her dress back up. She picks up the glass and takes a tiny sip.

"Wham, bam, thank you, Sam," the first girl says.

Her milk doesn't have a lot of flavor. It's a little sweet, maybe a little metallic. It might taste pretty good, mixed with some Kahlúa.

She opens the lid of the john and dumps the rest into the bowl. She waits for the two girls to go before she comes out of the stall.

A boyfriend, just for tonight. It sounds like a good plan. Kiss 'em and don't miss 'em. She leans over the bathroom sink, where someone has recently vomited. Diana better not come in here or she'll freak. Jamie puts on more lipstick and redoes her eyeliner. She looks older than eighteen, for sure. She looks good. Too good for the Lava Lounge, but this was where she'd wanted to come. The Lava Lounge, where Budweiser signs plaster the walls, where "Free Bird" is still on the jukebox, where nobody ever wears anything but jeans. She'll stand out. Finding a boyfriend should be easy.

Diana is at the bar, having her second cosmopolitan. She's getting drunk. It looks good on her; a little relaxing of the tension lines in her face, a little slouch in her usually straight shoulders. She's one tense lady. Rules up the ass: Clean this, don't let this touch that. Sometimes Jamie wants to slap her.

"Hey, girl," Jamie says, waving her glass. "Looks like I need another."

"I think I'm getting kind of tipsy," Diana says. "You know, I don't usually drink."

"Maybe you should."

"My mother's a drunk. I never want to be that out of control."

"That's kind of what I like about it," Jamie says. She scans the faces at the bar. The guys actually sitting at the bar are the loners, the losers who won't go home with anyone. They huddle over beers or shots, and occasionally look around the room, too shy to make any moves, hoping someone will come over to them. Jamie's been to the Lava Lounge a lot. She has a fake ID that says she's twenty-three. She hasn't been here since getting pregnant, though. Her mom had gone on and on about fetal alcohol syndrome. But now all bets are off. She wants to get trashed. Stella can stay on a bottle for a day or so, until Jamie's milk is alcohol-free again.

"Fill me up," she says to the bartender, who's new since she was here last. He's tall, pale, with lank blond hair that falls over one eye. His arms are thin and tightly muscled. He has a pyramid and eye, like on a dollar bill, tattooed on his right shoulder.

"Lemon drop, right?" he says.

"Jamie," she says.

He takes the glass. "Haven't seen you before."

"I used to come here."

He gets a fresh glass and runs a lemon wedge around the rim, sugars the rim, and sets the glass on the bar. He pours the vodka—a long pour—and Triple Sec and lemon juice and sugar in a shaker, and stands in front of her while he shakes it. She wants to climb up on the bar and mash her mouth to his. They can sneak into the storeroom and make out among the kegs and boxes. He'll shove her up against the cold steel of the walk-in refrigerator. She'll take off her sandals so he can suck her toes.

"How come you stopped coming around?" the bartender says.

"No reason." She shrugs. "No reason at all."

"I'm out of here by three."

"We'll see," Jamie says.

"Take it out of this," Diana says, indicating a stack of money on the bar.

Diana launders her money. Literally. She comes home from Teddy's World and puts all the bills from her wallet in the washer along with her clothes. Jamie's mom, who Jamie always thought was weird, is beginning to seem normal.

"This is my mom," Jamie tells the bartender.

"Hey," he says, taking some money off the pile. Then he goes to help someone else.

Jamie checks out the rest of the Thursday night patrons.

The pool tables are busy, as usual. Almost nobody looks appealing, and the boys that do look good have girlfriends. For the night, at least. The girls from the bathroom are over there. The sluts. Jamie realizes she knows them from high school. They were seniors when she was a freshman, and they were sluts then, too.

Jamie can't meet the bartender at three A.M., because Diana hired the sitter only until midnight. Stella will wake up during the night, and Jamie will have to be there.

The sluts, Jamie knows, have both had abortions. Now they can do whatever they want. They can screw those guys they're talking to, and stay out on the beach all night, and eat breakfast enchiladas and transparent hash browns at the Shore House Cafe at five A.M.

"Hey, you," a voice at her elbow says.

She knows who it is, even before she turns around. Anthony. Mercedes Man, whose leather backseat she probably wrecked forever by having a baby on it.

"Oh. Hi," Jamie says. Of all people, she has to run into him. He saw her half-naked, screaming her head off, another, smaller head sticking out of her. He saw her afterward, crying and shaking. He watched her being wheeled away, down the hall of the hospital, like a sick old person.

"I've been looking for you," Anthony says. "I went by your house and everything. Your mother didn't know where you were."

"You went by my house?" Jamie says.

"I had a good talk with your mother. She's quite a lovely woman."

"I guess," Jamie says. At the hospital, her mother had used the exact same words about Anthony. "He's a lovely man," she said. "I'm so glad he found you in time. He's still in the waiting room. Would you like to see him?"

"No," Jamie said. Her mom was so clueless.

"I called her today," Jamie says now, hoping that this news will shut him up.

"She was worried about you. Where have you been?"

Anthony is acting like some kind of cop. Maybe he is a cop. Jamie tries to remember what he told her about himself that day. He was wearing tennis clothes. Cops probably don't play tennis.

"Did you come here looking for me?"

"No, this is kind of my neighborhood bar. I live a couple of blocks away."

"I thought you didn't live here," Jamie says.

"I do now."

Anthony looks ecstatic to see her. He's shifting back and forth, hands in the pockets of his pressed black pants, smiling like he's crazy. Jamie remembers now; he seemed crazy that day he picked her up. What was it he said? That he had thrown his cell phone away. "We're all going to die," he said. Maybe he has a disease. He doesn't look like he's wasting away or anything. He's stocky and muscular, like her dad. Younger, though. He's like her dad was when she was little. When her dad could swing her in circles and take her for mint chip ice cream at Baskin-Robbins and make up stories featuring Jamie as a female astronaut. She went to the moon, and to Mars and Saturn. She made friends with the people there. It was a big disappointment, later, to discover that there was no one out there, that life on other planets didn't exist.

"Hello," Diana says. She's been sitting there not saying a word, just getting to the bottom of her drink in a hurry. "I'm Diana McBride."

"Anthony Perillo. Want another?"

"All right," Diana says. "Why the hell not."

"Anthony's the guy in the Mercedes," Jamie explains.

"Did the blood come out of your backseat?" Diana says.

"I don't know. I donated the car to the Police Officers Association."

"Why?" Jamie says.

"I'll tell you sometime," Anthony says. "I am so glad to find you. How's that baby?"

"Stella. She's fine. She's great. It's my birthday today."

Jamie feels like she has to explain to Anthony why she's here, in a bar, instead of at home with Stella. Maybe Anthony will tell her mom about seeing Jamie, out drinking and partying. When she called her mom earlier, her mom hadn't offered to babysit. No money, either. "Happy birthday, honey," her mom said. "I wish you the best." Her mom is cold and unfeeling; Jamie never realized it before.

Anthony waves the bartender over and gets Diana another cosmopolitan. He orders a Heineken and looks at Jamie. "It's on me," he says. "What do you want?"

"Lemon drop. But I just got one." She hopes he'll buy her one later. If he won't, though, Diana probably will. Or maybe, by the time she's done with this one, she'll meet a boy. Sometimes it's like finding an ATM machine; you can't find one right away, but there will be one in the next few blocks for sure. When you hook up with a boy, he might not dispense money, but he'll have something for you. A cigarette or a light, pot or Ritalin or beer, something to make sure you stick around long enough for him to make his move.

"It's her birthday," Anthony tells the bartender.

"Are you her dad?" the bartender says.

"Just a friend," Anthony says.

"Got it," the bartender says, and doesn't even look at Jamie.

Jamie tucks some fallen strands of hair behind her ear. Anthony has ruined it with the bartender. It was ruined anyway.

This birthday is starting to suck. It feels like she is out with her parents—OCD Woman and Mercedes Man. Anthony is nice enough, but she wants him to go away.

"I can't believe you gave your car away," Jamie says. "No car, no cell phone. Are you, like, becoming a monk or something?"

If he had only given his car to Jamie, she could have driven to New York by now. She could have gotten a car seat from Teddy's World and hit the road, and gone to see Leila. If Jamie and Stella couldn't stay in the dorms, they could sleep in the car.

"No way," Anthony says. "I got a new cell phone."

"What are you doing in Long Beach?" Diana says.

That's just what Jamie wants to know. She hopes he isn't stalking her.

"Just living," Anthony says.

"And . . ." Diana says.

"I lived in L.A., in Echo Park, until I was twelve," Anthony says. "Then my parents moved us to Maryland. I decided to come back to the West Coast. I rented a little place on the beach."

"So now you're like a beach bum?" Jamie says, bored, scanning the room again.

"I read the paper at a coffeehouse in the morning, pick up a game at the tennis courts most afternoons."

"Nice work if you can get it," Diana says.

"I used to own a dry cleaner's," Anthony says. "I just sold the business."

Jamie catches the eye of a boy slouching against the wall by the bathrooms. He was at a party at Kevin's house once. Troy Somebody. He puts his thumb and forefinger together and brings them to his lips and mimes toking on a joint, then jerks his head toward the back exit.

"Really. Dry cleaning!" Diana says, a lilt in her voice.

"Excuse me," Jamie says. "I'll be back in a bit." Diana and Anthony will be fine alone. They can discuss stains and mildew, chemicals and dirt. Underarm shields. They have plenty to talk about.

Jamie kills her drink and heads for the exit.

26

HOMEWORK: Keep a record of your exposure
progress.

THE Lava Lounge is dirty. The floor looks like there's a layer of scum on it, the bar rag is streaked and damp, the olives and tiny onion garnishes in their brown caddy are exposed to the spit that flies from people's mouths as they talk. I feel like washing, but that would mean going into the bathroom, and I think I'd rather not know what's in there.

I take another sip of my cosmopolitan, and another, and another. If Gloria could see me now, she'd be thrilled. We could bond over getting shitfaced. A strange man we'd just met, also shitfaced, could drive us home. He could dump us on the lawn next to the azaleas, and we could throw up next to them and then crawl toward the apartment together.

"Why did you sell your dry-cleaning business?" I ask Anthony Perillo.

He reaches into his shirt. He pulls out a gold chain, with something hanging at the end of it. Two somethings. Gold rings. "Here's why," he says.

"Are those wedding rings?"

"They're fused."

He leans in to show me. He smells like soap and some light cologne. Anthony is the cleanest thing in here, besides me.

"She died a little over a year ago," he says.

"I'm sorry."

"Hodgkin's lymphoma."

"That's not contagious, is it?" I can't help it. I have to ask.

"Cancer," Anthony says. "It develops in the lymph system. The lymph system is made of tubes that branch out all over the body. It's part of the immune system. So you can pretty much figure it out from there. She didn't even know me, at the end."

"How awful," I say.

"Her name was Eva," Anthony says.

"Eva," I say.

"Eva," he says.

I can tell that just saying her name makes it better and worse for him. I bet he could stand here all night, saying her name to strangers, conjuring up his dead wife for a two-syllable instant in which she shimmers in the air like lit neon before disappearing again, blinking off, just a dirty tube filled with gas. Alive-dead-alive-dead. I've done it with Tim—said his name over and over, like touching my tongue to a sore in my mouth.

"For a while I threw myself into work, or tried to," Anthony says. "Then, as it got closer and closer to the anniversary of Eva's death, I just hit a wall."

I'm not sure I want to hear any more of this guy's sad story. I look around for Jamie, but she's nowhere in sight. I hope she's not getting sick in the bathroom.

"So I decided to kill myself. I wanted to do it by the Pacific Ocean."

"How?" Now he's got my attention. Suicide: the ultimate obsession. No tiresome repetitive rituals, just a single act. Afterward, no more anxiety. For you, anyway. All the pain is left to the living. There's an elegance to it, at least in theory.

"I've got all kinds of pills from Eva's prescriptions," Anthony says. "I figured I'd unfold a lounge chair under the stars, wash the pills down with a good bottle of wine, and go out to the sound of the surf."

"Sounds lovely," I say. Except mentally I move the lounge; I drag it off the beach and leave it outside against the wall of my building, then go upstairs and shower. I take all the pills with water, and then I dial Tim's number. "See what you did," I tell him, and he listens as my breathing gets shallower and shallower.

"Then I picked up Jamie," Anthony says. "It was the anniversary of Eva's death. I was going to do it that night."

The thing is, suicide can fail. You wake up with half your face blown off from a shotgun, or you're lying on a table getting your stomach pumped, and the next thing you know you're committed to some filthy mental hospital with a bunch of droolers. You jump off a bridge, like people are always doing in San Francisco, and your ribs get shoved through your lungs but you somehow live, a pitiful, twisted creature in crippling pain, for another sixty years.

"I saw that baby being born," Anthony says, "and it changed everything. I looked at her and, I don't know." He tucks the rings back inside his shirt. The top two buttons are unbuttoned. His chest hair is black, and looks like little threads of silk. Tim had exactly seven hairs on his chest. Anthony's got some kind of tattoo I can just see the edge of—a C curve, like part of a heart.

"Something happened that day," Anthony says. "Something amazing."

"So what now?" I'm not even bothering now to put my drink back on the bar between sips. I just hold it. Sip, lower the glass a little, bring it back to my lips. So this is how it's done.

"How's Jamie's baby?" Anthony says. "Is she all right?"

"She's a baby. You know. She sleeps a lot. She cries."

"Eva wanted kids. I said we should wait. I wish we hadn't."

"Jamie should be back by now." I look toward the bathrooms

again, but no Jamie. I'm not sure I could walk a straight line anyway, so I decide to stay put. There's something about Anthony
that I like. His white shirt. His grief. The fact that he hasn't
asked me one thing about myself. I sense he could as easily be
saying all this to the man sitting next to me, a big hulk with
greasy long gray hair, his hands around a beer like he has to cool
them down with the chill from the glass.

"I'd like to see that baby," Anthony says. "What's her name?"

"Stella."

"'Stella by Starlight.' Played by Miles Davis. One more reason to live. Want another?"

I haven't finished this one, but he's already signaling the bartender. Hey, Gloria, look at me. A good-looking stranger is buying me drinks. If I were you, I'd be sitting up straight, crossing
one leg over the other, dragging on a cigarette and sizing him up
through the smoke. Trying to guess what kind of jewelry he'd
give me. Diamond, ruby, emerald? I'd be thinking.

But I'm not Gloria. I'm pulling down my black dress because
it feels too short. I'm worried, because I have to pee, and that
means facing whatever is in the Lava Lounge bathroom. I'm
thinking about how grotesque death is. Those jumpers off the
Golden Gate? If they succeed, their bodies are carried out to sea.
When they're found, crabs have eaten out their eyes and cheeks.
All the marine animals have taken bites. Death in general is unsanitary; the bacteria have a field day. You bloat with gas, you
turn green, you shit yourself. If there is an afterlife, I will probably, on arrival, look for the showers before seeking out my
dead grandparents.

"Drink up," Anthony says.

I do, and he takes my empty glass and hands me a full one.

The shape of a martini glass was permanently imprinted on
me from an early age. Joy. Fear. Love. Anger. Gloria.

"Chin-chin." Anthony touches his glass to mine.

The contamination travels from the soapy gray water of the bar sink, to the rag that wipes each glass, then to Anthony's glass. Now it's passed to mine. So what. As long as nothing has touched the floor. The floor of the Lava Lounge is truly scary looking.

"To the next step," he says. "Let's drink to that, whatever it is."

The next step is this. I take a big hit of my drink. I set the glass on the bar. Then I slide off my stool, and walk, with my heart beating very fast, toward the bathroom.

27.

IN her dream, Stella floats in the Light. Floats doesn't really describe it, because she's everywhere the Light is. She's inside it, but there is no inside. When Stella existed in the Light, there wasn't any language, but in this dream, she thinks in streams of words, and the words are all in different voices. There are bits and pieces of the TV news program the babysitter watched earlier, and snatches of courtroom shows and *Biography* and *E! Entertainment Television*—all the stuff Jamie watched while she was pregnant with Stella. Characters from several movies drift through, talking in Stella's head.

When I like a guy, the ceiling's the limit.

That was a movie Diana had rented. What did it mean? Where's the ceiling, where's the limit? Stella tries to look up, but it's dark up there. The movie was in black and white. Jamie wasn't crazy about black-and-white movies, she said, but she watched a couple of them for Diana's sake. Diana had seemed very sad, watching them. Diana didn't know about the Light. The Light is white, the world is black. The Before is blue. Don't put me in the black. The black is darkness and suffering. It's too hot or too cold. You're at the mercy of other people. Bad idea, the black.

The black was a hole and she fell into it, and came out of Jamie. She came out, and along with the other smells there was a cologne. Lagerfeld. There were men in blue, and a man wearing white shorts.

She didn't know who that was.

Before I was offered that part, Shirley MacLaine says, I had a dream about the opening scene where Aurora tries to climb into the crib.

Stella can feel the pad underneath her. She's in her bed. She can hear the TV in the living room. Jamie's not out there, sprawled on the couch. She's not here, lying on the futon next to Stella, filling the room with the fragrance of Coffee Body Butter and nail polish and vanilla candles. Jamie is gone. Jamie is being born somewhere. No, that's not it.

I want to be anonymous, Shirley MacLaine says.

What is it?

Blair's allies continue to blast him on Iraq.

Houston, we are venting something out into space. I can see it outside window one right now.

Music. A Chopin prelude. It's so sad she wants to cry; the sadness in the music, the sadness in the world.

Sharon left Ozzie over drugs. Britney is embracing the Kabbalah.

Take some responsibility, young lady, Judge Judy says.

Santiago might return to San Diego in '04.

There's a tiny door in that empty office. It's a portal, Maxine.

Stella tries to wake up. She feels paralyzed. This baby body is useless. Why can't she wake up? Why can't she move?

Fasten your seatbelt. It's going to be a bumpy night.

28.

THIS is killer weed," Troy says. "Be careful."

"I'll be fine," Jamie says, and takes a big hit. Like I can't handle it, she thinks. Like he thinks his weed is so awesome.

The alley behind the Lava Lounge smells like a cat has sprayed there, and also like the Mexican restaurant a couple of doors down. Lard and burritos and piss. From somewhere else comes the smell of burned coffee. The pot smoke wreathes around her, cutting through all that. She and Troy silently pass the joint back and forth.

When it's gone they just stand there. Troy rocks back and forth in his black Converse sneakers. He pushes air through his teeth, *sst sst sssst,* like he has a slow leak.

Jamie crosses her arms, leans against the dirty brick, thinks better of it, and paces a little in front of the red-painted metal door that leads back inside. There are hearts and initials and penises and a swastika scratched into it.

"Can you please stop doing that?" she says.

"What?" Troy says. He's wearing a black baseball cap with an "X" on it. He tugs it lower.

"Making that noise."

"What noise?"

"Never mind." She doesn't know if she wants to make out with some guy who hisses and doesn't even know it. But right now, Troy is the only candidate.

At Kevin's party, Troy sat on the broken couch the whole time, with a girl on his lap. The girl only got up to go get him beers; she went into the bathroom, where the tub was full of them, and came right back. Troy ignored her and watched TV, while she sort of slung herself around him—legs draped over his, arms around his chest, her head tucked under his shoulder. Jamie doesn't remember seeing them kiss. Maybe that was his girlfriend, and he won't want to kiss Jamie because he is being faithful to Beer-Fetching Girl.

"So what's up," Troy says.

"Not much," Jamie says. "It's my birthday."

"Cool." Troy looks off down the alley.

Jamie looks, too, but there's nothing there. Backs of buildings. Trash cans. Dumpster. Light post at the end of the block. This is her life. It is never going to get any better. She will turn nineteen, twenty-one, forty-five, and she will still be right here.

"Is there anything going on tonight?" Jamie says. "Any parties or anything?"

"Nah," Troy says.

Great. Jamie looks toward the Lava Lounge door. Might as well go in. Diana is probably wasted by now. Maybe Anthony can drive them home.

"I've got some X, though," Troy says.

Troy has Ecstasy. How long has it been? Too long, Jamie realizes. The last time was nearly a year ago, with Leila. They went swimming naked in Leila's pool in the middle of the night, ran naked across the lawn, and lay shivering uncontrollably in the grass. They blew gigantic bubbles from a ring the diameter of a dinner plate, rainbowed blobs that wobbled and drifted away toward the pool house. They wrapped themselves in beach towels and lay on the floor in Leila's bedroom with candles all around and listened to Ani DiFranco's *Out of Range* over and over, and drank seven bottles of Evian between them and took Ambien stolen from Leila's mother's supply to come down. It had been delicious, incredible, and perfect, but it couldn't last. Jamie was going to get pregnant and Leila was applying to NYU and a bunch of other schools.

If only I could go back, Jamie thinks. Close my eyes and just freeze time. She and Leila could live in Leila's parents' house forever, eating sandwiches that Graciela made. They could live there with the plasma screen TV that had all the premium movie channels, with the pool and hot tub and with Lawn Boy, who they both had a crush on and used to spy on from Leila's room while he rode the mower, shirtless, around and around the enormous yard.

"We could go sit on the beach," Troy says. He digs into his back pocket and pulls out a square of tinfoil. "Check it out." He unwraps the foil and shows her several oblong white pills. "Dolphins," Troy says.

The dolphins stamped on the pills are leaping. The dolphins are free.

Anthony will take care of Diana. After all, he had taken care of Jamie, when she might have ended up having her baby in the bushes somewhere. He is a responsible adult. He'll make sure Diana gets home.

"I can only go for a little while," Jamie says.

She can call from a pay phone somewhere and leave a message on Diana's machine. Diana will understand. It's not like Diana's an old lady. One night after watching a video, when they were dancing around during the credits, Diana had started doing a sexy sort of striptease, taking off her terrycloth robe and flinging the belt across the room, bumping and grinding in her T-shirt, running her hands through her hair. Then she had burst out crying and run into her bedroom. Diana will definitely understand.

"I can't stay out too late," Jamie says.

If Stella's hungry, Diana can feed her some formula. There's plenty in the fridge. Jamie will be home before too long, anyway. She'll just go sit on the beach with Troy for a while and make out with him. It'll be no problem, kissing Troy on Ecstasy. On Ecstasy, people are easy to kiss.

Ecstasy. They named it that for a reason.

"Just one," Jamie says.

"Happy birthday," Troy says, handing her a pill.

29.

HOMEWORK: Do not wash your hands more than
five times a day, thirty seconds each time.

SHARON said I had to start resisting the urge to wash.
Defer it for ten minutes, she said. Then another ten.
Then ten more.

Even if you feel very contaminated, don't wash.

Even if your arms go numb.

Look at your hands, how dry and cracked they are.

If you can't resist, she said, wash once instead of the usual
three times. Don't start with the thumb and work toward the
pinkie, like you usually do; change it up.

I don't let myself touch the toilet seat of the Lava Lounge
bathroom; I hover over it. There are no disposable tissue seat
covers, anyway. I hold my purse so it doesn't make contact with
anything—the floor with its chipped green tiles, the wooden
stall with hearts and phone numbers gouged into it.

There is nothing wrong with washing your hands after peeing. You're supposed to. There's even a sign in the bathroom:
EMPLOYEES MUST WASH HANDS. It's the law.

Fecal contamination, you can imagine. Even your urine,
though, isn't sterile after it leaves your body.

Only two thirds of people who use public restrooms wash

their hands, and women wash way more than men. Every time I see men shaking hands, I shudder.

I stand looking at the sink, but it's filled with vomit, and the smell of it makes me want to turn around and heave up my dinner and drinks into the toilet. I look at the plastic liquid soap container on the counter. Pro Pride Lemon Lotion Hand Soap. But the sink is too disgusting to go near. It's like a fire-breathing, bone-chewing dragon is guarding the hot water in the faucet, the pale yellow spurt of the soap. I can't get near that. Would Sharon be proud of me, for not washing, or disappointed that, once again, I couldn't bring myself to use a public restroom sink?

I step out of the bathroom and go through the motions of washing, rubbing my hands together. Nobody notices; it's gotten more crowded, and people are pressed closer together the nearer you get to the bar. The noise has ratcheted up a few levels since we got here. The jukebox is playing "Blue Sky" by Patty Griffin, a song I love, but I can hardly hear it. I look for Jamie in the crowd, but there's no sign of her.

I make my way to the back exit and push down the metal bar of the door. The alley is empty. Nothing to do but head back to the bar. I push my way through and find Anthony, in conversation with a little Asian girl in a blue tank top that says "Bitch" in silver glitter across her nonexistent breasts.

Asian girls never used to win pageants. Black girls, either. A black woman didn't win Miss Universe until 1977. Now they have a better chance. By and large, though, pageants are still racist, sexist events.

Needless to say, Gloria and I don't see eye to eye on this.

"You're in my seat," I tell the Asian girl.

"Oh, sorry," she says. She slides off the stool, and practically into Anthony's lap. He catches her and she sidles around next to him. She puts one hand on his shoulder, like she needs it to balance, but then she leaves it there.

"I can't find Jamie," I tell Anthony.

"She'll be back," he says.

The way he says it makes me feel better. He sounds so sure. I realize my response is totally irrational—how does he know?—but then again, repeated, ritualized washing is not exactly a rational response, either. I feel like Anthony has things under control, somehow. Maybe he didn't when he was planning to overdose on pills on the beach, but he's different now.

"Relax," he says. "It's still early." He turns back to the girl. "So, velvet," he says. "Moisture wrecks it. You spill a drink, it's all over. Chiffon, same deal. And chiffon catches on edges. Long formal gown and high heels? There goes the hem. Organza: yarn separation."

"Wow," the girl says. "I had no idea."

She rubs his shoulder, like she's appreciating the fabric of his shirt. She sips at something in a tall glass with an umbrella. Her lips on the straw are full and very red. Suddenly I'm afraid Anthony will want to go off with her someplace private, to discuss taffeta, and I'll be left here by myself. I don't want to be alone. Not tonight, and probably not ever again. I've liked having Jamie at the apartment, even with the baby there, even with my contamination issues. Somebody to post rules for. Somebody to talk to when I come home from Teddy's World. Another presence stirring the air, so the silence and loneliness don't crush me.

I understand now why old women always have cats, why Gloria has always had a man to live with and another stashed somewhere, like a reservist waiting to be called to active duty.

"Anthony," I say, "tell me more about Eva."

He immediately spins his stool my way. The other girl drops her hand from his shoulder and gives me a look. I give her one right back, and she takes a step away from us.

"Eva," Anthony says. "She was so beautiful. I mean, not in a conventional sense, like you. She had stick legs and big hands and she hunched when she walked, and her eyes were bad but she wouldn't wear her glasses in public, so she squinted. It made her look like she was scowling all the time."

Charming, I'm thinking.

"You really think I'm beautiful?" I say. "Conventionally, anyway?" Already I'm tired of hearing about Eva. Rest in peace. Tell me about me.

"This is something Stendhal said," Anthony says. "When you love someone, everything is further evidence of the beloved's perfection. Something like that."

I reach for my drink and discover I've finished it. This is all getting out of hand. Being in the Lava Lounge. Using that disgusting restroom. A dry cleaner quoting Stendhal.

"I've never read Stendhal," I say, impressed that Anthony has.

"Eva was a voracious reader," Anthony says.

The Asian girl, at least, has turned away completely.

"Eva introduced me to all kinds of great literature," Anthony says.

I could talk about Tim's taste in books, I guess, but I don't want to think about Tim. I don't want to think, period. I want to go home. I want soap worked into a white lather, swirling and shimmering on my skin, and very hot water.

"Eva taught high school English," Anthony says. "On weekends, she taught music to disadvantaged kids. She was great with kids. Practically the whole school came to her funeral."

Scalding hot.

"You know, you're a very good listener. I feel like you understand all this, somehow. Am I imagining that? Do I sound like a crazy man?"

No, I'm not. Yes, I do. No, you're not. Not any crazier than me.

"I guess we've all got our crosses to bear," I say. Brilliant.

Can't I come up with anything better than that? What would
Eva say? She'd probably quote Tolstoy. Flaubert. Thomas Mer-
ton.

"What's your cross?" Anthony says.

"You don't want to know."

"Aw, come on. Try me. I just talked your ear off about Eva."

The thing is, I want him to like me. I look into his earnest
brown eyes. One black lash above his left eye seems to be missing. There is a tiny blank spot there. I lean in close to him, and
he inclines his head. There is a small diamond stud in his left ear
and I know, without even asking, that it must have belonged to
Eva. I imagine her opening a black velvet box with the pair of
earrings glittering inside, an anniversary present, maybe. I imagine her lying in a bigger box, a satin-lined casket in the funeral
home, her lovely large hands folded over her breasts, her beautiful weak eyes closed forever, while Anthony leans over and
slips a single earring out of her ear and places it in his. Eva is all
over Anthony. She's a stain that won't come out no matter how
much solvent he uses. The Eva stain. Worse than butter, car
grease, red wine, indelible marker.

I put my mouth to his ear.

"I wash," I tell him.

30.

JAMIE pulls a big bottle of Dasani spring water from the shelf of the glassed-in refrigerator case at the 7-Eleven. She's already feeling the Ecstasy. Her body is lighter. Her cells are beginning to hum and vibrate. The rows of plastic bottles have a slightly glossy look. She takes a second one, for Troy, and goes up to the counter where he's ordering a cherry Big Gulp.

"Oh, me, too," Jamie says. She sets the bottles on the counter. The clerk is a big freckled boy from her high school. This town is too small; everyone she's seen tonight is from high school. When she is old, she will push her walker to the church for bingo and see the same people. They will all be buried together, according to what year they graduated.

"We'll all be buried together," Jamie tells Troy.

"What flavor?" the clerk says.

"What?" Jamie says. She crosses her arms and looks at the goosebumps on them, and starts shivering.

"What flavor Big Gulp," the clerk says, sounding superior and impatient. He has a deep, sonorous voice that doesn't go with his enormous round face or his tiny mouth.

"She told you cherry," Troy says.

"No, she didn't," the clerk says.

"You're such a dumbass, Carter," Troy says.

Jamie's teeth chatter. If she has a Big Gulp now, she thinks she may freeze solid. But Carter has already turned toward the machine to make their drinks. "It's cold in here," Jamie says.

"Here." Troy takes off his scuffed black leather jacket, hooks it on his index finger and holds it out to her.

Jamie slips it on. It smells like cigarettes and cologne. Boy fragrance, Troy fragrance. The lining inside is silk, or feels like it. She watches Troy take out his wallet and lay a twenty on the counter. It's one of the new ones recently issued by the Treasury, with the different colors on it. She never noticed how pretty the new twenties were. Troy himself is way cute, with his green eyes and smooth light brown skin. A pencil-thin black beard follows his jawline, a thin mustache edges his upper lip. Troy is so cool. He wears leather and has killer weed and Ecstasy. He is paying for the water and Big Gulps, not thinking twice about it.

Carter—he doesn't have any other name, that Jamie can recall—picks up the money and makes change and puts the bottled water in a bag, poor Carter who, she remembers suddenly, has some sort of heart condition. In school he was permanently excused from gym, and would hang around the library instead, playing chess with other outcasts.

"We're outta here," Troy says, heading for the door.

"Take care of your heart," Jamie says to Carter.

Carter looks at her. He stares at her breasts, and his tiny mouth falls open. He must eat a lot, to be so fat, but it seems impossible he could get much food into that little hole. "Okay, beautiful," he says.

Jamie grabs her Big Gulp and hurries after Troy. He's holding the door open, leaning against it, his head back, eyes closed. She passes through the door to the sidewalk and he doesn't move.

"Ready?" she says.

Troy slowly opens his eyes. "I'm fuckin' flying already," he says.

Jamie feels an incredible bond with him. They will fly together. They'll rise above the shitty earth and all its difficulties and go—somewhere. Where are they going? Where is anybody going, really? She glances back into the 7-Eleven and Carter is gazing after her. Poor Carter. His defective heart could give out any minute. One day soon he will probably be caught by the surveillance camera clutching at his chest with his freckled hands, collapsing to the floor. She has the urge to run back in and kiss him. He will be so surprised. When he is lying behind the counter, taking his last, labored breath, it is Jamie he will remember, Jamie's tender kiss.

But there is Troy, still against the door, and Troy is so cool. She moves toward him, leans in and kisses him. She falls into his slim chest and his open mouth and he tastes like red sugar and his tongue feels enormous touching her teeth and the roof of her mouth and it's so beautiful and she could stay here forever with him except that a man walking into the store goes, "Take it somewhere else, will you," and shoulders past them.

She pulls back; Troy's eyes are still closed. She looks into the store at Carter, who is staring at her with pure hate in his squeezed-together eyes.

"Come on," Jamie says. "Let's go to the beach."

"Yeah, the beach," Troy says. "It's a plan." He starts walking fast ahead of her.

It's easy to keep up because she's so light. Everything is easy. They get to the street corner and the signal changes that very instant. The glowing red hand on the opposite pole changes to the electronic white glowing walking man. The air pulses with freshness and the palms wave above them, alive, alive, alive. Jamie's never felt so in love. It was fate that led her to the Lava Lounge on her eighteenth birthday, fate that Troy was there and not somewhere else. He puts his arm around her as they walk and the energy flows from his arm into her side and radiates toward her heart, which is beating very fast. She's sweating now.

She takes a long suck of her Big Gulp and the cold rushes in and her head turns to a block of ice. The rest of her is warm. Melting. Or maybe not even there.

When they get to the beach, she takes off her sandals and runs. She spins in circles a few times, collapses, and lies looking up at the stars for what feels like a long time. The stars pulse; they are alive. Little lights zing from one to the other. Jamie tries to find some of the constellations her mom taught her, years ago. It doesn't look like there are any patterns up there, just a bunch of discrete glowing particles in the dark.

Troy has disappeared, for now, but it doesn't matter. Everything is perfect. A little breeze brushes her skin and the sand is soft as a bed, and the stars are so pretty and the waves sound like blood sloshing along her veins and arteries, *shush shush whoosh*. Ah.

Troy lays himself over her like a blanket.

"Hi," he says.

"Hi," Jamie says.

"Want to fuck?"

Jamie laughs. "No way."

"How about a blow job?"

"Kiss me," Jamie says. "You're a great kisser. Let's kiss. I love to kiss."

"Blow me," Troy says, "and then I'll kiss you."

"No way."

"Please."

"Maybe."

"Please."

"Okay." When he rolls off her, she feels like she's going to float right up.

He kneels beside her, his fly open. She gets on her knees, too, and then lowers her head toward him. He's soft and as soon as she puts her mouth around him, her gag reflex kicks in.

"Wait," she says. She tries again and it's the same thing.

"I think I'm going to be sick," Jamie says. She turns away from him and throws up. There goes the pan-seared pork loin with figs and roasted chestnuts in a vermouth reduction. Arugula salad, olives, bread. And the chilled dark-chocolate mousse. When she's done, she feels better, and even higher.

"Damn, girl," Troy says. "Am I that bad?"

"Sorry," Jamie says. "It wasn't you."

"Well I'm not gonna kiss you now," Troy says. "Not until you brush your teeth." He zips up and tugs at her hand. "Come on. Let's walk."

They stumble along the packed sand by the water. The ocean washes over her bare feet and over Troy's black sneakers. The beach is so beautiful. The world is so, so beautiful. Troy is a god, stopping to cup his hands around a lighter and cigarette, smoking as they walk, exhaling smoke, talking about his next tattoo. It's going to be a Celtic cross. Or barbed wire around a heart. Or a Chinese character that means "life." Maybe a snake.

"Snakes are so awesome," Jamie says.

"Full sleeves, man," Troy says. "That's what I want."

"Where are we going?" Jamie says. "Where is anybody going?"

"My place. You down with that?"

"I'm down with everything." She's not about to go back to the Lava Lounge feeling like this. No more going back. Just flying. A gull swoops by, low and to her left, over the ocean. Troy moves ahead of her, walking on the packed sand but out of reach of the waves. She slogs through the water behind him.

31.

HOMEWORK: Contaminate your living
environment.

I AM getting very anxious. The contamination from the
Lava Lounge bathroom is all over me.

There is no contamination, nothing is going to happen, I'm
going to be fine. It's all in my head.

"What do you mean, you wash?" Anthony says.

"Wash your hands before dinner," Gloria used to say. She
had no idea what I was up to, how many times a day I stood at
her bathroom sink, wearing her soap down to a transparent
sliver. My mother liked those flavored and colored glycerine
soaps—strawberry, peach, mango—and they didn't last as long
as regular soap. I was always buying replacement bars and
sneaking them in.

"Nothing," I say. "I don't know what I meant."

She knew about some of the counting, but she was supersti-
tious anyway, and I don't think she thought much about my
good and bad numbers. And the counting went away, after I
quit pageants. For a couple of years I was fine. Then one afternoon, in my senior year of high school, I came home from
school early, feeling sick, and went straight into the bathroom.
I was thinking that I should shower and clean off any germs

from school, because a bad flu was going around. I ended up showering for an hour. That night, before bed, I washed my hands for almost as long.

This is not the kind of thing you tell a stranger.

In fact, you don't tell anyone.

Even Tim didn't know, for a long time.

"You said you wash." Anthony's not going to let it go. Suddenly he's interested in me.

"What else did Eva like to do, besides read?" I say.

"Is it something you can stop?" Anthony says.

"Look, forget I said anything." I look around at the crowd, at the laughing, gesturing people gaily exchanging molecules and microbes.

Microbes are very good at adapting. Antibiotics kill them at first, but pretty soon they grow resistant.

"It's just dirty in here, and I wish I could wash my hands," I say. "The bathroom sink was filled with vomit."

"Eva had a brother," Anthony says.

I reach for my drink, relieved that we're back on the subject of Eva.

"He had violent thoughts all the time," Anthony says. "He thought he was going to kill somebody. He thought he might stab their mother, or strangle Eva. He imagined taking a power drill and drilling a hole through his father's forehead."

"How awful," I say. My arms are crawling. I look at them: nothing there.

"The thing was, he was a sweet, gentle kid who would never hurt anyone."

Nothing I can see, anyway.

"And one day," Anthony says, "when he was seventeen, he hanged himself in their parents' rec room."

"God, I'm sorry," I say.

"It always haunted Eva. And later she figured out he must

have been an obsessive, and she got kind of obsessed herself, reading about this stuff. Telling me how it all worked. Her brother would check the front door seven times when they left for school. He'd imagine he had run over someone with his bike, and she would go with him to the place he said he'd left a kid bleeding, and there would never be anyone there. She felt guilty that she hadn't known what was wrong, that she hadn't been able to help him. Nobody knew the worst of it until after he killed himself and they found these journals he kept. So," Anthony said.

There is absolutely nothing on my skin. I know that.

"So?"

"So you can tell me about it," Anthony says.

Just like that, I start to cry. "I can't," I sob. "I can't, I can't, I can't."

Anthony puts his arms around me. I bury my face in his shoulder, embarrassed to be crying in public, but I can't stop and probably no one is noticing, anyway. In a place like this, where everyone is busy getting thoroughly shitfaced, people probably cry all the time in the arms of people they have just met.

Drunk people cry a lot, I know from experience. Gloria introduced me to several of them. Gloria herself did not cry, but her friends did. They fell down a lot, too. Sometimes they set things on fire, accidentally or deliberately.

When you're drunk, you're liable to do anything. Dance topless on a restaurant table until you're kicked out. Scream at a pageant judge when your child doesn't make the finals. Take home a stranger whom your daughter will encounter in the kitchen next morning as she's standing on a stool, getting a box of Frosted Flakes from the cupboard.

The daughter will be in a T-shirt and underwear.

"I'm sorry," I mumble into Anthony's shoulder. "I don't usually drink," I say, pulling back from him and wiping my eyes.

"That's probably a good thing," Anthony says. He's handing me some napkins, each with a drawing of a red volcano.

The stranger in the kitchen? He'll say things to the daughter. Nasty things about what he'd like to do to her. The mother will come in while he's saying them, and hit him in the back of the head with an iron. He'll fall to the floor, bleeding all over the fake-brick-patterned linoleum, and won't get up. The daughter will spend some time with an aunt and uncle, while her mother deals with police and judges. When the mother comes back for her, the girl won't want to go.

"Maybe I should take you home," Anthony says. "Do you have a car?"

"Yes, but Jamie," I say. It's not like she can't walk from here; the Lava Lounge is two blocks from the apartment. But I don't want to ditch her.

"I'll take you home, then come back and wait for her."

"Okay." I'm in no condition to make a better plan. Home sounds good. Shower. Bed. Oblivion.

Stella.

"There's a babysitter at the house," I say. "She'll need a ride."

"Check," Anthony says, taking my arm, guiding me toward the door. He moves a little ahead of me to make a path through the crush of people. Anthony will take care of me, the babysitter, Jamie, everything. He's that type. I should have married a dry cleaner, I realize. Someone who would not leave me just because I was sick, because I had a problem in my brain. Someone who would stay until the end, wherever and whenever it came, and afterward wear my ring fused to his on a chain around his neck, and never, for even a fraction of an instant, forget how very much he loved me.

32.

STELLA has finally managed to sleep, but she jerks awake when the phone rings. There's an extension here in the room, with an answering machine. Jamie's not supposed to make long-distance calls on it, but she sometimes calls her friend Leila and then Leila calls her right back.

The babysitter, Karen, picks up the phone at the same time the answering machine clicks on, and her "Hello?" is amplified into the room.

"Hi." There's a pause. A giggle.

It's Mom.

"I'm not going to be home for a while," Jamie says.

"Who is this?" Karen says. "Is this Jamie?"

"This is Cleopatra, Queen of the Nile."

There's a boy's laughter behind her. Loud music. Jamie's voice floats above a techno beat. "Qu-eeeeen, of the Niiiiiiille," Jamie says. "Tell Diana."

"Tell her what?" Karen says, but there's a click. "Hello? Hello? Shit," she says, and then she hangs up, too.

The door opens, and Karen comes in and stands over Stella.

"You're awake. Poor little thing," she says, stroking Stella's wispy hair. "Doesn't sound like your mommy's going to make it home tonight. I think she's high," Karen says. "You know, kiddo, I think your mommy may be a bit of a fuckup. What do you think? Shh, it's okay. Go back to sleep now."

Stella squirms restlessly. She grabs onto Karen's index finger, but it's not much comfort. She knows Karen is right: Mom *is* a fuckup. Jamie makes bad choices.

But I chose her, Stella thinks.

Like mother, like daughter.

Who was that boy laughing on the phone? It wasn't Dad, that's for sure. Stella remembers Kevin's laugh. He copied it from Butthead, a cartoon character. Beavis and Butthead. Kevin could do a perfect imitation of Beavis, too. "I need some TP for my bunghole," he used to say, in a gravelly voice, and crack himself up.

This is no way to start out, Stella thinks. I love Mom, but she doesn't seem to love me back. Not enough, anyway. I make her too frustrated. Maybe I shouldn't have come down here in the first place.

Too bad it's too late.

Or maybe not.

Some babies don't make it. Stella has seen them. They're sucked out of the Before, but after a little while they come back. Sometimes, before they're even born on earth, they leave their mothers' bodies and are completely back in the Before. Others are alive down there, living on earth a few weeks or months. Something happens, Stella doesn't know what. It's not their time. When they return, they cluster at the far end of the Before, where it's a brighter blue. No one knows what happens to them after that. Maybe they go back to the Light, forever and ever.

They spark and are gone.

33.

HOMEWORK: Place your hands on a contaminated object. Practice the Calming Breath.

I REST my head on the passenger door while Anthony drives us back to the apartment. It's a very short ride, but I wish it would last forever, because I don't want to go home.

"What's the code?" Anthony says.

For a moment I'm confused. I fell asleep for a minute, and now we're at the gate of our building's parking garage. I tell Anthony the numbers. The gate slides open, and I direct him to one of our parking spaces. We have two, side by side, and the second one is of course empty. The ghost of Tim's Explorer sits there, idling, filling the garage with the poisonous fumes of memory.

We take the elevator up, and I unlock the door, which says "McBride" on a small tag under the knocker.

"Do you mind taking off your shoes?" I say to Anthony.

"Oh. Sure," he says.

I show him the laundry room just to the right of the door, and he puts his loafers on the plastic sheeting next to Karen's sneakers.

Even without Tim's things in it, the apartment reminds me of him. The plastic sheeting is where his shoes lived. In the kitchen is the refrigerator, with the shelves that held his beer. In the shower are the tiles he stood on in his bare feet.

If Tim hadn't left, none of this would be happening. I would be living my life right now, instead of reeling through this strange situation. Tim and I never had guests, for one thing, since guests might bring in contamination, and you couldn't exactly ask guests to change their clothes before they sat down. Now there is Stella, and Jamie due to return, and Anthony and the babysitter. The apartment is overcrowded. I feel claustrophobic just thinking about it.

Karen is sitting at the kitchen table with her laptop and an open textbook of some kind. She's going to be a physical therapist. She's going to make something of her life, because she was never beautiful and useless. She's a sweet, solid girl who probably never heard the words "Smile or I will smack you."

"Hey," Karen says. "Jamie called. She left kind of a confused message. I don't know if she's going to make it back tonight."

"Oh, okay. Thanks," I say. "This is Anthony. He's going to run you home."

I take out some money, making sure I give Karen the bills that were on the bar at the Lava Lounge. I smile, and ask about Stella, and act like it's no big deal that I'm about to be left alone with that baby.

Who might wake up, and cry.

Who might need her diaper changed.

Who might need me to pick her up and hold her.

"Thanks again," I tell Karen.

"Oh, no problem," she says. "She's a really sweet baby."

"Isn't she, though," I say.

"Can I see her?" Anthony says.

"Right through that door." I haven't gone in there since Jamie and Stella moved in. Once I stood in the doorway, and looked at Jamie's clothes all over the floor, and saw a dirty, shit-filled diaper lying on top of the dresser, and I backed out.

Anthony goes in.

I head straight for the master bathroom. I wash my left hand, thumb-index-middle-ring-pinkie. I wash my left arm, all the way up to the shoulder. Then I start on my right side. I rub the palms together, I interlace my fingers, I turn the water on as hot as I can stand it and hold my hands under the faucet until all the soap runs off, and then I start over.

I manage to do it three times before Anthony calls to me.

"Diana," he says, "I'm leaving now. Come say good-bye."

I dry my hands quickly and come out. Karen is standing at the door with her backpack and the leather shoulder bag that holds her laptop. Anthony is bent over the kitchen table, writing something on a napkin. A Lava Lounge napkin, and he's got it right on the table.

"Here's my number," he says, trying to hand me the napkin. I just look at it, and he lays it on the table. "Call me anytime," he says. "I really want to see that baby when she's awake."

She's sleeping, then. Good baby.

Anthony puts out his hand. "And you," he says. "I'm really glad to meet you."

I give him my hand and he holds it in both of his. My hand is red from the hot water. It's dry, as usual. I use a lot of Nivea, but it's never enough.

I try to pull my hand away, but he holds it tight.

"Call me," he says. "Okay?"

"I will." I have no intention of calling him, ever. I feel ashamed, just standing there. I know he knows what I have just done, in the bathroom.

Jamie, of course, knows all the rules, but she doesn't know how much I wash. She thinks I am excessively neat; she thinks I am kind of eccentric. She ignores half the rules, anyway, and I don't say anything. When she violates one, I pretend I don't notice, and then I break out a fresh bar of soap.

I feel like Anthony can see into my brain, like an MRI machine. He can see right into my basal ganglia, where they say the problem is with people like me. He can see that though I have been trying to do the homework Sharon gave me, I am failing miserably. I am not practicing again and again with each situation until my discomfort significantly lessens. I am not stopping any contact with water for days at a time, or even one day.

I am not capable of changing. This is who I am.

"Diana McBride," Anthony says.

I'm the Princess of Soapsuds. The Lather Queen. Crown me with a clean plastic bag.

"Promise you'll call," Anthony says.

Slip it over my head, don't let anything get in.

"Of course I will," I lie.

34.

TROY sits cross-legged on the floor, trying to light a chunk of hash with a Bic. He burns his thumb, swears, and then gets it going. After taking a hit, he passes it to Jamie.

When the hash is done, she goes to find the bathroom and a toothbrush. The first door she tries is Troy's roommate's; she pushes it open, and a curly-haired guy seated at a desk, wearing headphones and boxers, looks up at her.

"Sorry," Jamie giggles. Everything cracks her up: Troy's apartment with its red-painted walls, the deer's head hanging on a plaque in the dining room, the lack of furniture. There's no couch or chairs, no dining room or kitchen table, only a few scattered pillows. Even the TV sits on the floor and not on a stand.

The bathroom is the next door. There is only one toothbrush. She brushes for a long time, enjoying the mint taste of the Colgate, brushing her tongue and the roof of her mouth. She puts her face under the faucet, closes her eyes and lets the water run over her. The bottom of her dress and her underwear are wet and sandy from the ocean, so she takes everything off and leaves it on the dirty yellow rug and floats back out to the living room, naked. She feels like a sprite on a cloud in one of her mother's paintings. Iridescent fairy wings flutter and glitter on her shoulders. She takes out her hair clips and bobby pins and shakes her hair out as she goes.

"Wow," Troy says, and gets up. "This way," he says, and leads her back down the hall.

Troy's room is tiny. His bed is on a high platform, and there is a table underneath it with a mountain of clothing on top. What look like comics, or magazines, are piled in neat rows beneath the table. A bicycle hangs on one wall. Jamie climbs up the ladder opposite the bike, and dives into the sheets and blankets. She stares at the ceiling. It feels a little like being in a coffin, the ceiling is so close. After a while, Troy climbs up after her. Jamie sticks her head over the edge, and looks down at the tiny square of rug and some scattered CDs on the floor. Now it feels like she's traveling on a flying carpet, far above the world.

Troy touches her back and she rolls toward him. He presses his body against hers and his tongue is in her mouth again, and it feels, it feels—what does it feel like? Jamie realizes she's been trying to describe the sensation to herself, instead of just feeling. Why am I doing that? she thinks. Why am I always doing that, instead of just being in the moment? I'm in the moment right now. I'm high on Ecstasy and hash. I'm kissing Troy. His tongue is in my mouth. It feels, it feels—

"Wait," Jamie says. Troy's hard-on, which was against her thigh, is nudging between her legs, nosing around, looking for a way in.

"I can't do that," she says.

"Why not?" Troy rolls away from her and lies on his back. His dick sticks straight up. He takes it in one hand and starts stroking it.

"It hardly ever gets hard on X," he says. "Look at that. Wow."

It's beautiful, she has to admit. It's beautiful not because of Troy, but because of itself. The beautiful penis. The way it curls up like a little nesting animal when it's not hard, all wrinkled and sweet. The way it gets bigger by rubbing against her, or being licked, or just by being near something that excites it. How it fills with blood, or whatever it fills with, and the veins stand out, like now. It's as magic a transformation as she's ever seen: a worm turning into a hammer. A penis is an amazing thing.

"I took some Viagra," Troy says.

"I can't do anything," Jamie says. "I just had a baby."

"Hey, that's right. I heard Kevin got you pregnant. I thought you got rid of it."

"I had it," Jamie says.

"Bummer," Troy says.

Jamie looks at him. She can't see his face very well; there's a candle flickering down below somewhere, throwing up shadows. She watches Troy play with himself. He doesn't need her. He's got drugs, he's got his loft bed, he's got his right hand.

Her breasts are swollen and aching. She's got to express some milk again.

"Want to see something cool?" she says.

"Sure." Troy's eyes have closed; he opens them.

Jamie leans over him, puts her hands around her right breast, and massages toward the nipple. She squirts a stream of milk into Troy's mouth.

"Awesome," he says, putting his hand to his mouth.

"I have to go express the rest."

"Let me try sucking."

"No way." She is not about to nurse Troy. One baby is enough.

Is, in fact, too much.

"Do what you gotta do," Troy says. He lies back and starts playing with himself again.

Stella is probably awake right now, hungry and crying. She

is opening and closing her little hands, turning her head from side to side, the muscles of her mouth working. Jamie's beautiful baby daughter needs her mother, and her mother is not there. Her mother is a depressive teenager, who at this moment is messed up on drugs, watching a boy she doesn't know jerk himself off. Jamie sees it very clearly: Stella is better off without her mother.

Troy reaches for her hand and closes it around himself. With his hand over hers, he keeps masturbating. Up, down, up, down.

What a thrill Troy turned out to be.

"I'm going," Jamie says, pulling her hand away. She starts down the ladder, trying to remember where she left her clothes. Someplace yellow.

"Where are you going?" Troy says. "Damn, girl. You just got here."

"Away," Jamie says, backing carefully down the ladder. To the beach, maybe. Back to the Lava Lounge to meet somebody else. She can't go to Diana's like this. Not tonight.

Maybe not ever.

Stella needs someone who can really take care of her. Lots of people want babies; someone will want Stella, someone with money and a family. Jamie shouldn't have tried to keep her. No, it's all right that she tried to keep her, but now she sees she has to give her back. Like a dress you think is cool until you realize you never want to wear it, so you go back to Mania and trade it in.

She'll trade Stella for her freedom. She won't be stuck in Long Beach, with an infant and no money and no place to live except with a cleaning freak.

Troy's room looks weird in the candlelight. The candle is a dark cone set on a stereo speaker, and the wax is melting down the front of the speaker. Her mom used to sing her a birthday song about a candle. Something about blowing out the other candles, but there was one that stayed lit. *Aglow,* as the song put it. The usual crappy New Age stuff, about the love that's in your heart, wherever you may go.

35.

HOMEWORK: Practice daily, with sessions lasting at least one or two hours.

IMAGINE getting up in the morning and taking your usual shower before going to work. Imagine holding the soap in your right hand for a prescribed number of seconds, outside the stream of water so none of it gets on the soap. Imagine holding it in your left for the same amount of time. If you screw up, you have to start over.

Imagine washing yourself in a certain order: shampooing your hair first, then the ritual with holding the soap, then cleaning yourself: left shoulder, left armpit, left arm, left hand; right shoulder, armpit, arm, hand. Left breast, right breast. Stomach, vagina, backside, buttocks. Left thigh and calf. Right thigh and calf. Feet last of all. Always downward, against the flow of the contamination.

Rinse thoroughly.

Repeat.

Rinse thoroughly.

Repeat.

Imagine you get up early, so you are never late for your job; you hate being late. You arrive a few minutes early, every time; that's how well you have prepared. You are an excellent employee, though you visit the bathroom frequently. You explain that you have a pelvic disorder, and your boss nods understandingly. You keep a bottle of Nivea in your desk, or behind the counter, to try and keep your hands from being so dry. When you quit the job, claiming that you are pregnant, that you inherited money, that you are moving to Atlanta or Philadelphia or Portland, someone always throws you a farewell party. At the party you smile tearfully, saying how much you will miss everyone, the work, the place. Secretly your skin is crawling. You go home and finish selling everything in the apartment, or the small rented bungalow with the lemon tree in the backyard and, in the front, the flower garden you love. Irises. Dahlias. Four kinds of roses. You tell your husband the next place will be better, and because he can work anywhere, and isn't all that attached to the places you live, he says, Okay, babe. If it will make you happy.

Only it doesn't make you happy. It works for a while: sometimes you are almost normal. You shower just twice a day, you wash your hands a few times, but it doesn't dominate your life. You convince yourself it was that awful job.

The new one is so much better, until it isn't.

"What, again?" Tim says, each time.

But Tim loves you. You are his McBride. You're his princess, his beauty, his Rose Queen and Miss Tropicana, even if you never really were. He loves you and he'll move to Seal Beach, to West Hollywood, to a different part of Long Beach. If that's what you want, Diana. If you think it will help.

After a few years of this it's almost a joke, only it's not funny. You come home and say, "I can't take that place anymore." Tim turns away and says, "What the fuck, Di." He says, "What's wrong with you?"

So now I'm alone with this thing in my brain, this neural mistake.

And I'm thinking Tim was the one stable part of it, through all this moving around and changing jobs.

Stable, and maybe a little passive, now that I think of it.

It was easier for Tim to just go along. Tim didn't like static. He liked Guinness and whiskey and html and javascript and Flash. He liked listening to the Pogues and Clannad, and visiting Mexico to buy folk crosses and Day of the Dead figures and Valium. He didn't like dealing with my shit. He didn't like having to shower before we made love. It was easier to pretty much stop touching me. We started making love only on special occasions—birthdays, holidays, our anniversary. Kind of like buying a Hallmark card at the Rite Aid. Getting something because you have to, not really caring what it says as long as it's got the basics right: Congratulations. For Your Special Day. To My Loving Wife. Stroking my breasts, kissing me, then asking me to turn over. Saying "Baby, baby" in my ear. Not "Diana, Diana," the way he used to. He stopped coming up behind me to put his arms around me while I stood at the kitchen sink. He stopped saying "Let's dance" and "Come here" and "You're so fucking adorable." No more rose petals in my mouth.

Imagine this is the marriage I'm mourning.

36.

I'M fucked up, Leila," Jamie says.

"I'm going online, sweetie," Leila says. "Just wait."

"I can't leave," Jamie says. "But I have to."

She's sitting at Troy's roommate's desk, using his phone. The roommate is nowhere in sight, but his computer is booted up. The screensaver shows two women in tiny thong bikinis, their backs turned, their asses exposed.

An Outlook Express icon is at the bottom of the screen and she clicks on it.

"JetBlue to JFK," Leila says.

"Stella will be all right," Jamie says. "She's with Diana. And Mercedes Man."

"Of course she will. You think my parents raised me? No way. I never saw them, and I got along just fine. When I was little, I called Graciela Mama. My first language was Spanish."

"It's just so hard having a baby," Jamie says. "I never knew it would be so hard."

"We'll figure it out. Can you open his mail program? I'm going to send you the receipt."

"She's better off without me."

"You have to give me the guy's e-mail address."

"Wait. Shit, I'm so fucked up. Wait. Okay. Morpheus80 at hotmail."

"Coming your way. Click on 'Send & Receive.'"

Leila's voice is calm. Leila always knows what to do. Jamie loves Leila more than anyone on earth. She misses her so much she can hardly stand it.

She needs more water. What happened to that bottle of water? And how does this guy's printer work? She turns a circle in his office chair, her head tilted back. Maybe she should just go back to the beach and lie in the sand again.

"Sweetie?" Leila says. "Do you see it?"

Focus, Jamie. Open the e-mail. Now click on "Print." Nothing happens. Okay, find the printer. There it is. Turn it on.

Maybe go find Troy and the magic carpet. Troy's tongue on her nipples. She needs them sucked very badly.

"Got it," Jamie says.

"Can you get to the airport?" Leila says. "Get that guy to give you a ride. If you go right now you can make it."

"Leila, don't go," Jamie says.

"I have to get off the phone so you can go to the airport. I'll see you soon."

"No. Don't go."

"Soon," Leila says.

Jamie clicks the phone off. She's still naked. She wanders into the living room, where a tangle of tiny white lights is blinking in a pile on the floor, and watches them for a minute. She goes into the bathroom, finds her heaped clothes next to her tiny purse, and puts them on. She is flying to New York in her new Betsey Johnson dress full of sand.

"Troy," she says, going back to his room. "Take me to the airport."

The candle has gone out. There's a strong smell of jasmine incense that makes her gag, and she thinks she might get sick again. Why does everyone like incense? Jamie hates it. Sticky, heavy, cloying incense. She stays in the doorway, talking to the darkness in the upper left corner where Troy is.

"What the fuck," he says. "I'm toasted."

"You have to," Jamie says.

"'You have to,'" Troy says in a high voice. "You sound like my mom." He comes down the ladder. "Just let me find my pants. Man, I hope I can drive."

He clicks on the overhead light and Jamie backs away from the glare. In this light she can see he has acne on his forehead. He puts his baseball cap back on, tugging down the brim. Boys have insecurities, too. Kevin hated his slim hands; he thought they were girlish. He had calcium spots on his teeth, so he tried not to smile. She had once thought he was serious, someone who had deep thoughts, but he was only hiding his teeth. She knows Troy isn't as cool as he tries to act. There is probably a cooler boy in New York, a boy she doesn't know but will meet once she gets there.

Troy owns a purple Hornet that used to belong to his parents. He drives nervously, like an old lady, hunched over the wheel. When they get to the big traffic circle where cars whiz in from the radiating spokes of the streets, he goes, "Fuck, fuck, fuck," under his breath. He cuts somebody off as he enters it, speeds up and shoots safely out a street on the other side.

At Long Beach Airport he misjudges the curb, and the front right wheel runs over it, then bounces onto the road again. A security guard on the sidewalk looks at them.

"We're busted," Troy says, panic in his voice. "Hurry up, get out. Act normal."

"Thanks for the ride," Jamie says. She leans over and kisses his cheek.

"No problem," Troy says, mustering up some semblance of indifference again. "Hey, happy birthday."

Jamie had forgotten. "It's my birthday," she says.

"See you around," Troy says.

She gets out of the car. The security guard has lost interest and walked away. Troy drives off, an uncool boy in an uncool car going back to his apartment, or maybe back to the Lava Lounge to find a girl who will do more with him than Jamie would. She goes in to the JetBlue counter and gets the tiny piece of paper that is her boarding pass, then waits with a handful of people to go through security. They are outside, in a walkway with blue plastic sheeted over it. It's a tunnel and she is trapped in it. When she gets to the electronic doorway she's sure it's going to beep like crazy, set off not by metal but by the chemicals in her brain. Amazingly, it doesn't. No one can tell that she is high on illegal drugs, that it's her birthday, that she is leaving her baby. She picks up her purse on the other side of the X-ray machine and goes into the women's room. She looks in the mirror and can't believe her own beauty. She's glowing all over, her hair is wild around her face, her eyes have a crazy light in them.

I look like a rock star, Jamie thinks. A brunette Courtney Love, before she lost her sense of style and got into designer gowns. I wish I had a jacket to take to New York. I should have worn one tonight. The frayed Levi's one that I put patches and embroidery on. That's such a cool jacket. I shouldn't leave that behind.

She'll send for her clothes once she's settled in New York. Or have Leila do it. Or something. Better not let Diana know where she is.

If Diana doesn't want Stella, she can take her to the adoption agency. That's what was supposed to happen anyway. Jamie's mom was right; she's not old enough to handle it. She's only eighteen. Girls just want to have fun.

Someday Jamie will come back to Long Beach, a famous rock star. Or maybe not, since she doesn't play any instruments or sing very well. But a famous clothing designer: she could definitely do that. Jamie can sew anything. She's always altering the stuff she gets from Leila, making it more interesting. Putting zippers in T-shirts, redoing dress seams, gluing things on shoes. She'll make clothes for famous people and be profiled on *E!* Entertainment Television, and somewhere, in an orphanage or foster home, Stella will see her and be so proud.

"That's my mom," Stella will say. "The bitch who abandoned me."

37.

STELLA can hear Diana crying in the living room. Who cares about Diana? She wants that guy Anthony to come back.

When Anthony came in to the bedroom Stella knew right away who he was. He was the one who had stopped for Jamie in his car. His cologne smelled familiar. Is he coming back? Where did he go?

He smiled down at her, touched her head.

"Hello, Stella," he said.

Now there's nobody here but Diana. She's crying and crying out there. Grown-up crying sounds bad. It must be those big lungs. Also Diana is talking to herself, but she's sobbing and hiccuping too much for Stella to make out the words. Someone should burp her, Stella thinks. What's Diana's problem, anyway? She doesn't have to lie around in a wet diaper until somebody comes along to change her. She can talk, and get her own milk when she wants it. She can roll over of her own accord.

Stella felt funny when she saw Anthony again. Her heart started clenching in her chest, like someone was squeezing it. He put his warm palm against her cheek. He was just a man-shaped shadow in the dark, but she knew who he was. She wanted her glasses so she could see him better.

I'm a baby. I don't need glasses.

How do I know I'm a baby? she thinks. Does a cat know it's a cat? Does a bird know? When do we become conscious of the fact that we're going to die? I don't want to die. I've hardly had a life yet. It all goes too fast, music played at the wrong speed, allegro when it should be andante. It all needs to slow down. Relax, don't try so hard. Slow and fluid, so it's all part of the whole, not individual notes. Try it again.

She sleeps for a while. When she wakes she feels feverish all over, and realizes she's sweating. A lot. She's peed herself and needs to be changed. How humiliating, to be in diapers. To have someone coming in, pulling back the sheet, changing you. Rolling you over, wiping you, cleaning up your mess. The body is a mess. Why do we want so badly to live in it? The body will betray you, every time.

Now there's no one here. I'm so alone. Does it matter who we love, or how much, if we're ultimately alone? Why love someone, when you're just going to lose them?

Time to cry, but for some reason she can't. It's like earlier in the evening: She can't move. She can't make a sound.

Something is wrong. She hurts all over, the pain sears through her, she doesn't know how she can hurt this much and still be alive.

Help me.

38.

DON't put that in your ear, Madison, that's an owie," the woman says.

It figures, Jamie thinks. Hardly anyone on the plane, and I'm behind a mother and her kid. She shifts in her cold leather seat, pulls an airline blanket over her and stares at the little TV screen. There's nothing on yet; they're sitting on the runway. Jamie can see the kid through the space between the seats, squirming on her mother's lap. How old is she? Jamie tries to guess. More than one, but less than two. The girl has dark hair put up in pigtails, little butterflies on the elastics. Her mother is wearing a red baseball cap with her ponytail threaded through the back of it. Maybe she, like Troy, is hiding acne. Maybe she's running from something, like Jamie is—a creep of a husband, or a damaged one like Jamie's father. Maybe she's sick of looking into eyes that seem to wildly, desperately want to say something important, while only nonsense comes out. Jamie doesn't know how her mom can stand to take care of her dad.

The little girl turns her head sideways and looks through the seats at Jamie. She gets out of her mother's lap, stands on her seat, and looks over the back.

"Hi," she says.

"Hi," Jamie says.

"Hi."

"Hi."

"Leave the lady alone, honey," her mother says.

The girl drops her pacifier in the gap between her seat and the window. Jamie leans down and picks it up.

"She dropped this," she says, handing it over the seats to the mother.

"Oh, I'm so sorry. Thank you." The mother is much older than Jamie. She waited until she was ready to have her baby; she planned it all out with whoever she is married to. She took her Estrostep every day until it was time to stop and have a family.

Leila is my family, Jamie thinks. My real family. The other one sucks. Your friends are the ones who matter. Blood families are just the people you grow up with until you're old enough to get your driver's license and a credit card and get away from them.

As the plane backs out from the gate, the woman pulls the girl back onto her lap. The girl makes noises behind her pacifier. "Ah-haaaaaaah," she goes, over and over.

Jamie closes her eyes. She's still pretty high. Now she's going to get even higher. She's never been on a plane before.

"Suck on it so your ears don't go bad," the mother says. "Oh, that's yucky water, we'll get you some new water." The girl starts crying.

Jamie looks out the window as the plane taxis down the runway. A plastic Passenger Safety Information card has passed from the seats in front onto the floor by her feet, but she ignores it. The mother tries to shush the girl but she only gets louder. Obviously, taking care of Stella wasn't going to get any easier. It's good Jamie left when she did.

"One, two," the mother says.

"Three," the girl says.

"Four."

"Seven."

At least she's stopped crying. The TV is showing a picture of an airplane over a map of a few states: Washington, California, Nevada, Arizona, New Mexico. A strip at the bottom keeps a running tab on speed and altitude: 239 m.p.h. 6658 ft. Then it switches to a Shop Blue screen advertising gifts. Blue umbrella. Blue tote bag. Blue baseball cap. Blue teddy bear.

"Five, six, seven," the mother says.

310 m.p.h. 9400 ft.

"I have Mickey," the girl says, squirming to look at Jamie again through the seats.

"What?" Jamie says.

"Mickey Mouse," her mother says.

Jamie hates Mickey Mouse and all things Disney. Her parents took her to Disneyland when she was seven. She was jostled by the crowds. On every ride, she was terrified. She dripped ice cream on her favorite red coat. If she were staying around to be Stella's mother, she'd never let Stella have a Mickey Mouse doll.

"Mickey Mickey Mickey Mickey Mickey Mickey," the little girl says. "Mickey Mouse. Mickey Mickey Mickey Mickey Mickey Mouse in the house."

Jamie hates children, too. She never realized until now.

"That rhymes," the girl's mother says. "You're such a poet."

This is who I would have been, Jamie thinks.

319 m.p.h. 9796 ft. Jamie looks down at the lights of greater Los Angeles. It's like someone has rolled silver glitter body gel up and down along the coast, next to the black ocean. If aliens passed by earth, they would see this from their starship and think that an amazing civilization had populated the planet.

They would think the people here must be a really evolved species, to light up their cities like that, to send all that flash and brilliance into the night, visible for miles and miles. Too stupid to know any better, the aliens would want to come here.

366 m.p.h. 11,206 ft.

They would think the earth was a beautiful place to live.

39.

HOMEWORK: Continue the program until you have successfully confronted the most distressful situations or images on your list. If you do not confront the situations that evoke the highest distress, it is more likely you will lose the gains you made.

APPARENTLY cosmopolitans have the same effect as Valium: very destabilizing. I wipe my face and blow my nose and, just when I think I've got it under control, another sob comes up from somewhere and I start crying again. Crying: such a pathetic response. It's one thing to be that little infant in the next room—who incidentally, I am happy to report, has not made a sound. It's another thing to be a grown woman, doing this regressive babyish shit just because she's got a few drinks in her. That is the only reason I am like this right now. I don't plan to cry over Tim ever again.

Put a lid on it, Gloria would say.

Gloria, as I said, never cried when she was drunk. She laughed, she danced, she was the life of the party. Then she broke things and passed out. The next morning, when she woke up, she asked for a Pepsi and a cigarette. It was my job to bring her those things. I brought her liquor, too. She always had a deal with a nearby store owner. For my mother, men broke the law. They sold me Merit Ultra Lights and Crown Royal and Skyy and Tanqueray. They handed me gifts for her, flowers and truffles and bracelets. Men like the chase, honey. Let them think they might catch you.

The more I think about her, the less I want to cry. I hit the couch pillows instead. I punch them and imagine they are a thin old woman in false eyelashes and heavy makeup and an expensive pantsuit. Then I go get the phone and dial her number.

She picks up on the first ring. "What?" she says.

"It's me."

"Oh," she says, sounding groggy. "What time is it?"

"It's late, I think. I'm sorry to call so late." I take a pen from the coffee table and make a note on the back of a Business Reply Mail for the Interstitial Cystitis Association. *Tim is a shithead.* The note is kind of scrawled, because I'm so drunk. I probably won't be able to read it in the morning.

"What is it now?"

"I'm sick," I tell her. "I have a problem with my brain."

"Holy fucking hell," she says. "What is it? Do you have a good doctor?"

"It's not like that. I have this—thing," I say. "I feel like everything's contaminated, and I wash all the time to get rid of the contamination. That's why we moved so much, and I changed jobs all the time. That's why Tim left me."

There's silence at the other end.

"Mom?" I say. "Gloria?"

"I saw something on TV about that. It's not serious, is it?"

Now I feel like crying again. "You don't get it, do you? You never get it." What did I expect? I expected some kind of catharsis. Gloria would say, "Oh, honey, I never realized," and I would be relieved of the terrible burden of my secret. A new under-

standing between mother and daughter. Closure at last. Cine-
matherapy theme song. Cut to commercial for Pampers Custom
Fit Cruisers.

"Get what?" Gloria says. "Are you blaming me for this?"

I wish I could. The research shows it's pretty much a biolog-
ical thing. Abnormal neurochemical activity. Less white matter
in the brain. I could have had the sweetest mother in the world,
and still I'd hear a bar of soap calling my name: a siren song lur-
ing me toward being dashed on the rocks, while I was tied to the
mast, eyes closed, listening to huge waves slapping the sides of
the ship.

"I just wanted you to know," I say. "I never told you, and I
just wanted you to know."

"Well, now I know. You're still my daughter."

"But you're disappointed in me."

"As long as we're speaking frankly," Gloria says, sounding
wide-awake now, "yes, I am."

"Because I stopped doing pageants."

"You had something special. You had a light in you."

"I could sing, I think. I felt like I could sing." I'd taken voice
lessons, but quit them when I quit competing. "Maybe I should
take some lessons."

"Maybe you should see a doctor about this brain thing.
Whatever it's called."

"I was, but I stopped."

"So start again," Gloria says.

"I got drunk tonight," I tell her. "I went out and got really
drunk."

"I can tell. Go sleep it off."

"Gloria—" I say.

"What."

"Stop criticizing me." I hang up before she can get in a comeback. She's right, though, I should go to bed. The house finch,

or whatever bird is impersonating it, calls out the hour. Tim didn't take the clock, after all. It's midnight, and Jamie isn't back. Midnight: the witching hour. Cinderella's deadline. Her dress is turning to rags, the coach is a lousy rotting pumpkin. The footmen are rats, carrying the plague, scurrying toward me. I look toward the room where Stella is sleeping, and it's dead silent in there. Good. I don't want to go near that baby if I can help it. I head for the bedroom. I want to shower, but I'm too tired; I crawl in between the sheets and move to the middle of the bed and wait to pass out.

40.

B EFORE Stella, before the Before, there was Eva. Baby
Eva, crawling across the orange wool rug in the living
room of the house in Bethesda, Maryland, crawling toward her
big brother, Noel. Noel held her hands so she could stand up,
wobbling on her baby legs, before she fell back onto her butt.
Noel's arms were strong and tanned, with light-blond hairs that
made it look like they were glowing when the sun caught them
just right. The living room was bright and he didn't let her fall,
and the next time she stood up he moved backward so she could
stagger forward.

Eva learned everything from Noel. How to walk, and later
how to ride a bike and blow perfect smoke rings in the garage,
and how to make a kamikaze from the ingredients in their parents' liquor cabinet. Which were the best books to read. Their
parents read John Grisham and Michael Crichton and Danielle
Steel. Their parents were nice people. Eva's mother worked for
the phone company and her father sold business machines,
which used to be typewriters but then became computers. They
were such nice people that they never talked about anything
real or important, but it didn't matter, because Eva had Noel,
and she could talk with him about life and boys and God and
shopping and evil. She could tell him anything.

She thought Noel could tell her anything, too, but she was wrong.

The day he killed himself she had skipped her classes at Thomas Pyle Junior High with her friend Amy, and they got Amy's brother Mike to drive them to Montgomery Mall. Amy bought a paisley blouse and a charm bracelet and stole a tube of Cherry Chapstick, and Eva wound a red silk scarf around her neck and walked right out of Hecht's with it, and later she would think about that a lot because that was around the same time Noel was taking a length of nylon rope and climbing up on one of the metal bar stools in the rec room. At the food court at the mall they had pepperoni pizza and Diet Coke, and then they went to the movies to see *Blade Runner*. Eva fell in love with Harrison Ford, whom she hadn't liked all that much in *Star Wars*. She imagined him saying "I want to put my hands on you," the way he did to Rachel, the replicant in the movie. She and Amy waited an hour for Amy's brother to take them home, but he never showed, so she finally took the bus home, still feeling floaty and romantic from the spell of the movie, and when she got there the ambulance had already come and Noel was already dead, and Mrs. Richardson from across the street was in their living room crying and her parents had gone to the morgue. And after that Eva found Noel's journals, which her parents didn't want to read, but she read every one of them.

When she met Anthony a few years later, he was selling jewelry at a kiosk in the mall and dealing pot on the side. She bought a pair of turquoise earrings, and then a quarter ounce. They didn't date. She just moved all her things into his one-bedroom apartment, and they started making plans to get married. Anthony's father owned a dry cleaners and wanted his son to take over the business eventually. When a friend of Anthony's got busted, he decided maybe that was a good idea, so he quit selling pot and went to work in the store. Then his father died, and Anthony continued to run the business. He did dry cleaning for senators and congresspeople and lobbyists and a couple of TV stars, and Eva taught at Sidwell Friends in D.C. and they were mostly happy and always and forever in love and maybe that's why she had to get sick and waste away, she thought sometimes at the end, because only in fairy tales was it ever any different. She hated dying on Anthony, because she knew he was stubborn and wouldn't want to find someone else; she knew he would carry his grief for years, and that made it worse, and she felt angry because of how it was going to be for Anthony when she died. And then she didn't know him, he was a stranger who came and looked at her sadly and who sat sobbing beside her bed. And then she died.

The Story of Eva. The End.

Stella sees it in little flashes. She thinks if she can see it all maybe she can go back and fix it. She doesn't know how, it's just a feeling she gets, that she can't explain. She has to pore over every detail. She'd forgotten everything until Anthony came and stood over her bed in the dark, until he leaned down and touched her hair with his warm and somehow familiar palm. For an instant she knew who he was. Then she didn't know anything, but after a while she saw the orange rug and then Noel in the front yard with his knees hooked around a tree limb, upside down with his plaid shirt falling over his face, and Anthony shaking a bottle of champagne and the white froth running over his wrist, and the black hairs on his chest that she loved and her mother saying "Set the table, Eva," and her father carrying a big box that held a computer and everyone watching it like television after he set it up in the living room. She saw the piano she played when she was little, an ebony Chickering, and the upright that she had in the living room of the apartment she and Anthony lived in. There was an ugly vase on top of it, a yellow glass vase with barbed wire around it and an image of a buf-falo, that her mother had given them and that they felt obliged to keep on display.

Noel's funeral—she sees that. It was snowing and they went to a church, St. Jane de Chantal. Kids from Noel's school were milling around and hugging each other and pointing at her and whispering. That's his little sister. God, I can't believe it. Why would he do it? That is so fucked up. After the service they all drove out River Road to a small cemetery and stood around shivering. They watched the box being lowered into the ground on some kind of hydraulic thing and everyone threw clods of freezing dirt on top of the shiny wood of the coffin and that was what became of her lovely brother, and what became of her, Eva—she was buried next to him, her flat marker set in the ground next to his, and their parents hadn't even died yet.

A feeling of wrongness about it all comes over her. Again she can't explain it. Is it wrong to be here? Where is here, exactly? She doesn't know. She's hot. She's soaking from sweat and urine and she's alone in the dark. And everything hurts so much.

In the Before—

Before what?

Before I was here.

Are there two of me now?

I want to be with Anthony.

I want my mom.

Someone needs to come and help me now. Why isn't there a nurse, holding a clipboard, saying Hi hon, how are you feel-ing? The hospital smells bad. Maybe it's her smell, her own sick-ness. Everyone here is sick and someone has to come and help them, help them even if they are getting worse and there is nothing anyone can do but someone should be there, it's too lonely to go through this without anyone.

But no one is coming, it seems, no one is ever going to come.

41.

JAMIE feels like she's dreaming. I am in New York, she keeps thinking. I am in New York with Leila, eating New York blueberry waffles with New York butter pats and syrup, and the waitress has a New York accent and those are skinny New York trees with their leaves turning yellow outside the window. New York, everywhere I turn. Wow.

She hasn't slept. The Ecstasy kept her up through the whole flight, and the little girl in front of her cried and fussed until just before they landed, when she fell asleep in her mother's lap. Jamie kept her blue headphones on, with the volume turned up, and watched TV. She's exhausted now, but so what. She's in New York.

"I am so happy to see you," she tells Leila.

"Girl," Leila says, digging into the last of her French toast, "you have got to sort this all out."

"Let's not talk about it yet," Jamie says.

"Whatever you say. I'm happy to see you."

"I missed you so much," Jamie says. The waitress comes by and refills her coffee without asking, dropping a couple of half-and-half creamers on the table.

"You have to meet Chris," Leila says. "And Shay. Naima. Dakota." She rattles off more names of people Jamie doesn't know.

"Cool," Jamie says, though she doesn't really care about Leila's friends. It's just so great to be sitting here with her. Leila has a new piercing in her left ear. She's cut her long hair to just the edge of her jawline, and dyed it blond, and of course it suits her. Leila's hair has been every color of the rainbow, and it all has suited her.

"My roommate, Darla?" Leila says. "She said she'd stay with her boyfriend for a couple of days. She hates the dorms, and we hate each other. So it works out."

"That sounds great," Jamie says. A couple of days? What about after that? Leila seems to think she's just here for a visit. A little time to chill and get her shit together. Leila doesn't understand that Jamie's left for good.

"You can go to classes with me today if you want," Leila says. "Or just hang in my dorm room if you're tired. I've got class until noon, then rehearsal. We're doing a performance next month. After rehearsal, some of us are meeting for drinks. You can hook up with us then. You can come to rehearsal, too, if you want."

"Great," Jamie says.

"Then tomorrow?" Leila says. "I've got classes, but I'll cut the afternoon ones because they're just academic stuff. I have to go to dance in the morning, though. But after that we can do whatever we want."

Jamie pops the creamers and stirs them into her coffee, then takes a few swallows. There is not enough coffee to erase this tiredness. She doesn't want to sit in classes all day. She doesn't want to spend the day alone in Leila's dorm room, either. But at least, in the dorm, she will be able to sleep for a while. She'd like to sleep all day, in fact.

Her breasts are hurting. The fucking milk again. Letdown, it's called.

"I'll be right back," Jamie says. She makes her way to the end of the diner, past all the New Yorkers reading the *Times*. They are on their way to jobs, or to classes, like Leila. No one looks at her. In New York, apparently, a girl in a short black Betsey Johnson dress in a diner at nine A.M. doesn't rate a glance. She goes into the bathroom and turns the lock, pulls her dress over her head and hangs it on the hook inside the stall. She expresses her milk into the sink, which has brown stains in the enamel. How long until her milk dries up? She has no idea. Knead, squirt, knead, squirt, squirt. It splashes in the sink and slides down toward the drain. Thousands of miles away, Stella is crying for it. Feed me feed me feed me. *Help me.*

"What?" Jamie says. She looks at herself in the mirror. A bumper sticker plastered to the bottom of it says ANGRY AMPUTEES. It's not her birthday anymore. The birthday glow has faded, leaving a haggard teenager with bluish half-moons under her eyes. Courtney Love on heroin, looking like shit, wasting her youth and talent. Kurt and Courtney, fucked up and nodding off. At least Courtney had Kurt, until he blew his brains out.

I have Leila, Jamie thinks. She dries her nipples with a paper towel. She washes her hands and face with gritty Boraxo from the dispenser, puts her dress back on, and goes out. Leila is at the register paying their check.

"I don't want to be late," Leila says. "So, what do you want to do?"

Jamie wants to lie down and sleep forever. She wants to wake up as Leila, with blond hair and money in her wallet and friends named Chris and Dakota, and classes to take and some reason to put one foot in front of the other.

"I'll just hang in your room for the morning, if that's cool."

"Okay. You can borrow some clothes," Leila says, looking her over.

Clothes. Jamie wants Leila's clothes, too. Tank tops and Seven jeans and T-shirts saying "King Moving and Storage" and

"Burlesque Review: Tenacious Tina" in pre-faded black letter-ing. New York is shopping heaven. *Sex in the City,* the ultimate fashion show, is shot here. There is one more season to go. Jamie wants to see Sarah Jessica Parker, as Carrie Bradshaw, walking down the street in Manolo Blahniks and an obscenely short dress the color of her skin that makes it look like she's naked. She wants to see Carrie's friends, sweet Charlotte and in-dependent Miranda and slutty Samantha, linking arms with Carrie. And she wants Carrie's on-again off-again true love, Mr. Big, to drive by in his shiny black car and roll down the smoked-glass window and catch sight of Jamie looking good in her new dress. "Abso-fucking-lutely," he will say.

Jamie looks out the window, but no one famous is passing by. There's a group of schoolgirls in checked uniforms and white knee socks, an old lady walking her poodle, men in busi-ness suits. There's a Starbucks on the corner across the street. It looks just like the Starbucks on Second Street.

"We'll go out after my rehearsal later," Leila says. "We'll cel-ebrate your birthday. It'll be fun."

Eighteen years from now, Jamie thinks, Stella will be old enough to look up her adoption records. She will see "Jamie Maria Ramirez" next to "Mother's Name" on the birth certifi-cate, and she will finally have a name to go with her years of longing for her real mother. She will leave the other mother, the one who will have fed her and taken care of her and bought her clothes for school every year, in order to track down Jamie in her New York apartment. "Why did you give me up?" Stella will say. "For fun," Jamie will tell her, and Stella will get a hurt expression on her face, but then she will say, "That's okay, Mom, I forgive you. I understand. At least you didn't dump me in a trash can or a Dumpster as soon as I was born, like some teenagers would. You tried, you really tried. You kept me three whole weeks. Mom, it's totally cool."

Jamie tries to imagine how Carrie Bradshaw would describe things. Carrie would sit cross-legged in bed with her laptop, tapping out her column while wearing something adorable. "When it's no fun being a girl," she would write, "do girls just wanna have fun?"

"Jamie?" Leila says. "Yo. Earth to Jamie."

Help me.

"What?" Jamie says.

Leila is standing there with her arms crossed, tapping her foot rapidly. "You are so spaced," Leila says. "Come on, I'll put you to bed."

They head outside, and Jamie wraps her arms around herself. New York is colder than Long Beach. The air is damp, the sidewalk is wet. Torn leaves are glued to it. In New York, she will need warmer clothes. She'll need a job and a place to live and a bunch of other shit she has no idea how to get. Leila has started off ahead of her, walking fast, and Jamie hurries to catch up.

42.

HOMEWORK: Write a story that describes in detail the situation, your actions in the situation, and the disaster you imagine will happen if you don't wash or clean.

I HAVE a new admiration for Gloria. I had no idea that when she woke up each morning, calling for her Pepsi and cigarettes, she felt this bad. It must have taken great determination to feel this way every day and still drink. Alcoholism, I see, involves perseverance on the part of the drinker. There are probably a lot of wannabe alcoholics who just can't cut it, who get up one day and realize they don't have the strength of will or the constitution to continue. They find an AA meeting, and from then on all they do is talk about drinking, too spineless to actually take another sip. I am one of the spineless; I don't wish to sample alcohol ever again.

The first thing I have to do is shower. I have to wash away the Lava Lounge, the cosmopolitans, the anxiety about Jamie's whereabouts. Maybe she's home by now. Maybe Anthony found her and brought her back while I was sleeping, and she's in there now, in her messy room that stinks of baby shit and Desenex and vanilla. I hope so, because I have to go to work.

I have to scrub off the image of Anthony, his kind eyes, his white shirt with the rolled sleeves. His forearms were tanned and muscular, from tennis I guess. Tim's arms were pale; they never saw the sun. He went running early in the mornings, then stayed in, like an animal in a burrow, an animal with an expensive sound system and a computer and CD burner and webcam. Right now, he is probably living on deliveries of pizza and Chinese food, without me to do the grocery shopping. I am not going to be able to wash away the twelve years of my life with him. Washing as a strategy is completely useless. Right shoulder, right armpit, right arm, right hand: wrong, wrong, wrong, wrong. But I can't stop. By the time the hot water's used up—which takes a very long time, in my building—I feel a little better.

After coffee and Advil and two packages of instant Quaker Oats, I think I might make it through the morning without throwing up. There's no sound from Jamie's room. I keep looking at the door and thinking I should see what's up. The northern oriole—or who knows, maybe it's a vulture—says it's six-thirty A.M., which means I should be leaving for work in an hour.

As long as I don't go over there and look in, I can imagine that Jamie is peacefully sleeping on the futon, next to her baby. It's like that famous paradox in physics that I never really understood, where a cat and poison are put in a box and the cat is either alive or dead in there, but you don't know until you look, and somehow looking is supposed to determine the outcome. But the cat's looking, right? The cat knows if it's alive or dead. Maybe I've got it mixed up with the one about the tree that falls in the forest.

I'm still trying to remember the scientist's name when another bird calls seven o'clock. I'm getting sick of hearing those

cheery calls day and night. I'll ship the clock to Tim. No more
singing birds for me. What is there to sing about? I want a clock
that moans in pain, that shrieks and sobs and weeps. Somebody
probably manufactures it, with Munch's *The Scream* on its face.
That's the clock I want.

Usually, by this time, Stella is wailing away in there.

I go over to the door, open it slowly, and look in.

No Jamie. The futon's covers are pushed back in a heap; she
never makes her bed. The floor as usual is covered with clothes.
Glamour and *Cosmopolitan* are on the floor just inside the door,
next to a bowl from the kitchen that holds a spoon and a residue
of chocolate chip ice cream. I can see the plush elephant mobile
from Teddy's World that hangs over Stella's bassinet, but from
here, I can't see Stella.

Schrödinger, I remember. Schrödinger's Cat was the big
paradox.

I listen hard, but there's no sound from over there.

I feel like there's a swamp between me and that baby. A
swamp of contamination, waiting to suck me in. All those
things strewn on the floor, they might as well be alligators. And
I have to walk right through them, because I know something
is wrong.

"Stella?" I say. I feel stupid, calling her name, because I'm sure
she has no idea yet what her name is. I'm thinking, though, that
maybe she'll hear my voice and make some kind of sound.
"Stella? Little baby? Hey, you. Are you okay?"

Nothing. I feel my hands and arms prickling.

Tim would probably come over, if I called and begged him.
If I told him what was happening, he would come. He's a good
person. A good man is hard to find. That's a quote from some
writer, I forget who. I bet Eva would know. Eva was a good person, too, I'm sure of that.

I'm sure Tim would get in his Explorer and break the speed limit, if he knew it was something potentially serious.

I am not going to sink that low.

I am going to cross the room.

Any minute now.

43.

JAMIE crawls into Leila's narrow dorm bed and pulls the covers over her head. There's still some sand in her dress, gritty on the small of her back. Sand in her underwear. The little grains of Long Beach sand, still clinging, hanging on. She's too tired to do anything about it. Her skull feels like there are cracks in it, fissures her thoughts keep falling into. The bones in her body feel like they've separated slightly from each other and need to be squeezed back together.

"Shoot me in the head," she moans. "I am so fried."

"I've got Xanax," Leila says. "And Ambien. I've got Ritalin, too, but you definitely don't want that. I raided my mom's stash before I left home. All your pharmaceutical needs." Leila puts a book in her leather backpack, followed by a shiny blue leotard and a pair of black dance shoes. "I've got Luna bars if you get hungry," she says, taking one from a stack on top of the small refrigerator tucked under a built-in shelf. "There's beer and vodka in the fridge, and some Thai noodles you'd better smell first to see if they're okay. I've got Snapple Lemonade and smoked Gouda and Gruyère and crackers. Don't touch the SnackWell's or Darla will have a shit fit."

"Give me an Ambien," Jamie says. Leila is a good hostess. She has everything. One day Leila will have a big house, like her parents, along with live-in help to cook and clean and raise her genetically superior children. It occurs to Jamie that maybe she, Jamie, could be the live-in person. She has all kinds of experience, from helping out with her father to cleaning Diana's apartment. She even knows a little about babies. Leila would pay her a good salary, and every so often—not too often, because it's bad for your brain—they could take some Ecstasy and lie naked on the grass in back of Leila's new house and laugh, just like old times.

"Here you go," Leila says, pulling the covers off Jamie's face. Leila hands her a pill and a bottle of sparkling water. "Gotta scoot. See you later. Sweet dreams."

"Leila," Jamie says, "you're the bomb."

"Love you, too, babe." Leila slings her backpack over one shoulder, grabs a striped scarf, does a pirouette, and swirls out the door.

Jamie sits up, leaning back against the pillow and the wall, swallows the pill, and takes sips of the water. Leila's side of the room has a framed poster of Isadora Duncan, a collage of photos of her and her friends shellacked to a board, and black-and-white postcards of probably famous women clothespinned to a line stretched taut above her bookshelves. Jamie recognizes Marilyn Monroe and Frida Kahlo, and nobody else. Darla's side is decorated with pictures of fairies. Above Darla's bed, on a wrinkled, curling poster, Tinker Bell trails a wake of sparkling glitter. Her pose is pure cheesecake—bent over with her hands on her knees, thrusting her fairy butt into the air above Peter Pan. A ceramic sprite rests thoughtfully on a rock inside a glass waterball on Darla's desk. On the calendar above the desk, fairies swarm inside a pink cumulus cloud, looking like Technicolor flies. Jamie's mother did the drawings for that calendar. The identical one hangs in their kitchen at home, with her mother's tiny red-inked notations of doctors' appointments for Jamie's father. On Darla's calendar, the squares are blank.

Jamie closes her eyes and waits for the Ambien to take over. She sees the squares of the calendar, the days she has to fill. It's a little grid floating behind her eyelids, a blue grid with no neat red lettering, no words, nothing but black space between the lines. Then the lines blur and turn into a blue nova that pulses and gives off little sparks, and then she feels her grip on the water bottle loosening and opens her eyes and sets it on the floor by the bed. She curls under the covers and closes her eyes again, and this time the blue shrinks to a tiny pinpoint. She waits for it to vanish completely and then she's floating above it somehow, and then she loses track of it somewhere in the blackness.

44

REMEMBER: Subtle avoidance reflects a reluc-
tance to give up your symptoms completely and
will hinder your progress.

WHAT would happen if I didn't wash? The rats would
swarm over me. The dirt and germs and dust would
cover me. I would disappear beneath a viscous wave of garbage
and filth.

What would happen?

Nothingness.

Nothing.

I go into Jamie's room, to the bassinet. The baby doesn't
look like she's breathing. I touch her forehead and she's burning up, which I figure must mean she's still alive; if she had
died, wouldn't the body be cool? How the hell should I know?
I pick her up. I hold her against me and stroke her back through
her T-shirt. She is so tiny and light I can't believe it.

"Okay, Stella," I say. "We're going to do this now." I carry her
hot, limp body out to the living room. I keep one hand cupped
under her bottom, touching the disposable plastic diaper, which
I can tell is carrying a full load. I wonder how long it's been since
she was changed. The babysitter must have done it last night
sometime.

This is so gross.

This baby is asleep, or dying, I don't know. Should I call an ambulance? Does Jamie have any insurance? Where is she, anyway?

This is not my job.

I did not sign on for this.

I am going to kick Jamie out, if she ever makes it home.

I carry Stella into the second bathroom, the one Jamie uses, and with one hand pull a towel off the rack and wet it with cold water. I carry Stella back to the living room, drop the towel on the arm of the couch so I can use my free hand to pull the afghan off the back and cover the cushion with it before laying her down. Being a mother, I see, is like being disabled. It makes you a one-armed amputee. No wonder Jamie's depressed.

Stella lies there with her eyes closed and her legs drawn up a little. Her lids look so translucent I feel like I can almost see her eyes behind them. She has a broad little nose and full lips; her lips are a deeper pink than the rest of her face, which looks pretty flushed at the moment. I still can't tell if she's breathing, so I lean down close to her.

It's kind of faint, but it's there, slow and shallow. I pull her T-shirt off and undo the diaper, pulling away the sticky adhesive tabs, turning my head away while I slide it out from under her. I can't believe a creature this small can make so much disgusting waste. I want to run right outside and toss the diaper in the trash chute down the hall, and then shower; my hands and arms are crawling. But I think I'd better get the fever down. I put the diaper on the floor; I'll deal with it later. I should have grabbed a fresh one from Jamie's room, but it's too late. I use the dry part of the towel to clean the baby down there as best I can, and then I use the other end to spread the dampness all over her face and down her body, her little chest and thin legs—aren't babies supposed to be fat?—

again and again. She shudders a couple of times and then goosebumps appear all over her.

"Stella," I say. "Hey, Stella."

I'd better call the hospital. I don't know what I'm doing, really. Stella will die, and Jamie will come home and kill me. Stella still hasn't opened her eyes. I leave her on the couch and go for the phone in the kitchen. On the way, I see the napkin with Anthony's number on the dining room table. In another minute I'm listening to his phone ring—five, six, seven times. Doesn't he have a machine? Who is this person?

I should have checked on this baby hours ago.

If only I were an obsessive checker, and not a washer, I would have been in that bedroom every two minutes. I would have gone back again and again, unable to trust my memory.

The doubting disease; that's what doctors call this. You can never be sure.

I am sure of one thing right now: if Anthony doesn't answer, I am going into deep panic.

"Yeah," he says, picking up finally.

"It's Diana. Jamie didn't come back last night. Stella is hot and I've been wiping her down. I don't know what to do. I think I better call the hospital."

"I'll be right over. I'll take you to the emergency room."

"She's shivering now. I don't know what to do." I've run back in to look at her and she's practically vibrating off the couch.

"Wrap her in a blanket," Anthony says. "Meet me downstairs, in front. I'll be there in five minutes." He hangs up.

I pull the afghan around the baby and bundle her in it, then pick her up. There's no time to wash properly. No time to get off the contamination from Jamie and Stella and that filthy diaper. There's no time to call Marlene and tell her that I will be late, or possibly not be in at all. I have to go back into Jamie's room and find a clean diaper and get it on the baby and find my purse and put on my shoes and go downstairs. Marlene will understand. Or she'll fire me. Or maybe make Kelly Employee of the Month, out of spite, even though Kelly doesn't deserve it. I can't worry about any of that now, because I am busy trying to save a life.

45.

THERE are so many things to remember. Stella sees the memories sliding by, a stream of faces and colors and rooms, and she puts her hand in and scoops up an afternoon—ice skating on the frozen canal by the Potomac, around and around until it got dark and the trees were black and her fingers were frozen inside her gloves. Or she gets hold of a gesture. Anthony pulling off his dark green T-shirt, the taut muscles of his stomach, the T-shirt hiding his face for an instant before he took it all the way off and moved toward her. Just that moment, or a series of moments: walking on the slimy bottom of a cold lake, then swimming out to a floating raft, and the heat of the boards. She lay down in her damp bathing suit, until it was dry; then she dove back into the shock of the cold again. Propped up in a bed, sucking water through a straw, the glass held to her lips—that was her; no, that was Eva. All of that was Eva.

Eva is dead; there is no more Eva. It makes Stella so sad she can hardly bear it. This is what happens. In the Before you see how it will be on earth, a little, but you don't really understand. You're still fresh from the Light and everything exists all at once, so what's the problem? You don't know the meaning of the word "problem." You just feel this urge to—to feel. You think some feelings will be bad, but probably not so terrible you won't be able to handle them. You think others are going to be amazing, and you focus on those and want them, after a while, more than anything. In the Light, love wasn't something you wanted or needed or thought about because it wasn't separate from you; there wasn't even a word for what you were. Stella can see now that if there was a word, "love" is close to what it would be. And then she started to feel it instead of be it; she floated in the Before and loved Jamie, scowling, unhappy Jamie with the purple polish flaking off her nails and her hair hiding her face, and soon they would be together.

But now Jamie is gone, and Eva is in the ground, gone.

And the memories stream past and Stella can't catch them; they keep rushing by, voices singing and crying and talking, and then they're gone.

This must be why some of the babies go back. In their mothers' wombs, or in their cribs, they suddenly understand. It's all about loss, this place. It's all about pain, and maybe you don't, after all, want to feel that.

But Noel shouldn't have left, he should have tried to live. And Eva—every minute of her twenty-nine years she wanted to hold on to life. She didn't want Anthony to give up.

The need for the new love *is* faithfulness to the old. That was a line from a poem she taught her kids at Sidwell Friends. The poem was about suicide. It was called "Wait."

Stella feels dizzy.

Who am I now?

Where are we?

My name is Eva. I don't want to die. No, that's wrong. I'm dead.

We're dead?

I don't know. I think we're dying.

What do we do now?

Wait.

46.

I N Jamie's dream, her father is out in the courtyard of the apartment building where they lived when she was little. He's laying tile over the cement, setting the squares carefully and grouting the spaces between them, working the way he used to. It's black marble tile, gleaming in the sunlight, transforming the drab courtyard into a ballroom. Jamie comes out of the apartment door and she can glide across the tiles like they're slick glass. She glides right over to her father, and even though she's grown now he lifts her easily, under her armpits, and holds her above his head and sets her on his shoulders. She's laughing and shrieking while he turns in circles. She's got her ankles locked across his chest and her arms around his neck, holding on. From somewhere she can hear her mother's voice, calling to him to stop, but he doesn't. He staggers once and almost falls but then they're spinning again.

When he finally slows, everything still spins: the mustard-colored walls of the building, the windows and narrow iron balconies, the scraggly bushes trying to grow out of gravel at the edges of the courtyard. Jamie's father puts her down and she stands, dizzy, looking down at him; somehow he's grown smaller. He's only as high as her knees, and her head is up there around the sixth floor.

She bends down—it's so far down now. She scoops him up

and holds him. His head falls back and his eyes look at her, then slowly close. His tongue hangs out of his mouth like a dog's, like Buffy's tongue did when she was panting. Jamie rocks him, and sings a birthday song he once taught her. *My name is Zoom and I live on the moon.*

Jamie kneels on the tiles and lays her father down. He curls on his side, and then is still. She starts pulling up tiles; with a little effort they pop off. Underneath them there's no cement anymore, just dirt. She begins digging with both hands; it's hard to make much progress, the dirt is hard and dry and full of little rocks she keeps pulling up and throwing aside. She feels as though she is going to have to dig forever. Finally she makes a hole big enough for him. She lifts him carefully, and puts him inside the hole. She looks down at the dirt on her hands, then at the mess of rocks and scattered tiles she's thrown aside. She looks toward their apartment door, but her mother is not there. It's gotten dark outside while she worked. Their apartment is dark. All the windows of the other apartments are black rectangles. There is hardly any light to see by, but she can see her father, lying quietly, not moving.

"Daddy," Jamie says, "do you want me to cover you up?"

"Gaaa," he says. "Airplane. Scissors. Pigeon."

"What?" Jamie says.

47.

Keep in mind that you may not experience
immediate improvement.

T HERE'S a sign by the receiving desk in the emergency
    room that suggests you tell the doctor how much pain
you're in, on a scale of 1 to 10. When I was seeing Sharon, she
had me make a chart of situations that made me anxious, on a
scale of 1 to 100.

In pageants, every girl got a number. Every girl got a score.
Several scores, actually.

Everything, apparently, can be quantified. If you are injured
in an auto accident, you get a certain amount of money for each
limb you lose. Your life is worth money, and your house. Pain
and suffering: there are dollar amounts to be negotiated.

By the time we got Stella here, she had stopped breathing.
The nurse took one look at her, muttered, "Shit," under her
breath, and suddenly Stella was taken away from us and hustled
off through a door, leaving us to sit here.

On a table in the waiting room there's a *Marie Claire* from
July with Claire Danes on the cover. "6000 Men Confess Everything You Ever Wanted to Know." "7 DAYS TO A SEXY BODY."
"725 SEXY FASHION FINDS."

Sitting in the emergency room, degree of distress: about 95.
All around us are people who are ill and possibly contagious.

An old woman a few seats down is coughing, not even covering her mouth, not using the handkerchief balled in her hand. A boy sitting with two others keeps saying, "I think I'm gonna heave, man," but he doesn't make a move toward the bathrooms; I'm waiting for projectile vomit to hit me in the face. I draw my feet up from the grimy linoleum floor. I wish Tim hadn't taken his Valium when he came back for his stuff; I could use one now.

"How are you doing?" Anthony says. He puts his arm around me and squeezes my shoulder. His hand is square and solid and warm. He doesn't bite his nails or his cuticles; there's no dirt or grease that I can see.

"I should call in to work," I say.

"Just breathe," Anthony says, "and it will get better."

He's right. I should be doing a few Calming Breaths right now. But I don't want to take any deep breaths in here. I don't want to inhale any germs. I'm breathing as shallowly as I can.

"I'm fine," I say.

"No, you're not."

"Look, I don't want to talk about this." I hunch forward and wrap my arms around my knees, and he takes his arm from around my shoulder. I pick up the *Marie Claire* and open it, and what appears is an article titled "The Secret Lives of Men." "Is your guy hiding a gay past? Sleeping with prostitutes on the side?" I close the magazine. My guy's secret: "My Wife Is a Washer." Only he's not my guy anymore.

Everyone has a secret life, don't they? Show me an average-looking person and I'll show you they're definitely hiding something. That well-dressed woman who used to come into Liquor Barn for bottles of Junipero Gin, and King Eider premium dry vermouth with the little etched crown above the label, an eider standing on an ice floe—she wasn't throwing fancy martini parties every few days. Marlene and her drunken comas in the back room of Teddy's World. Dr. Woo, the dentist I worked for, was sleeping with his married hygienist. They'd go into one of the exam rooms sometimes and close the door, and I'd hear their muffled moans while I called patients to confirm or reschedule appointments. A couple of times before Tim left, we went to see a marriage counselor, but then a performance artist whose website Tim designed said she'd seen the therapist at a sex club in L.A., tied with ropes to a cross. After that we went back only once more, and the whole time he was talking about communication skills I just looked at him thinking, You had yourself hung on a cross.

I wonder what Anthony's secrets are, and I hate him knowing one of mine. I only told him because I was drunk. One more reason to stay away from alcohol: it makes you honest.

"You don't have to be ashamed of it," Anthony says. "I can help."

"I don't know if I want help."

"Yes, you do."

A doctor comes into the waiting room. Stella's not with him.

"Did you bring the baby in?" the doctor says, looking at me.

I can't answer. I just look at him. I know what he's going to say. We tried, he'll say. We just couldn't get that little heart started again. So sorry. My own heart freezes.

"Yes," Anthony says.

The doctor smiles. "We're going to keep her for observation. Probably overnight. We don't know what caused this. But I think your baby's going to be all right."

"She's not our—" I start to say, but Anthony says loudly, "Thank God. Thank you."

"You can go upstairs and see her," the doctor says. He comes over and shakes Anthony's hand. The doctor is young and handsome, with a square jaw and deep green eyes and blond hair, like a character on a soap opera. He gives me a reassuring smile, showing his upper teeth, two of which are capped. I can always spot them, from working for Dr. Woo. Teeth have numbers, too. Amount of gum recession, that gets a number.

Relief that you have not let someone's baby die: priceless.

"Take care," the doctor says, then heads back through the door.

Anthony turns to me and hugs me fiercely. "She's okay!" he says. "She's okay!"

His hands are warm on my back. His arms press against my ribs, squeezing me. I can't remember the last time anyone hugged me like this—like they really needed to, like they weren't going to let me go.

"Stop it," I say. "Please stop."

He does, abruptly. I take a step back, and nearly step on the sneakers of the coughing old woman. She's got her feet thrust in front of her like she's trying to trip me, to make me fall on the germ-filled linoleum.

"Watch it," she says. "You think you're the only one?"

"One what?" I ask her.

"The only one," she says again. She coughs at me, and I turn away. "Let's go," I say to Anthony. "Please. Let's get out of here. They're keeping her overnight. We can come back and get her tomorrow."

"I think we may have a problem there," Anthony says.

"Why?"

"They might not let us take her tomorrow. I mean, the paperwork."

"We filled out the paperwork," I say. Anthony did, anyway. I gave him Stella's full name and birthdate, which I knew was the day Jamie first came into Teddy's World. I had him put down my address, and write "None" on the insurance information, and he signed to be responsible for paying the charges.

"They'll probably have to release her to family," he says. "We aren't family. We don't even know where Jamie is. They could get Social Services involved."

"We know where Jamie's mother is, though."

"Let's go pay her a visit."

"Anthony, I have to go to work." I think about Mary Wagner-Ramirez's house, about her feet with their long nails, and the mutant cat. "Can't we just call her?"

"Nope," he says cheerfully. He actually looks happy. He must be one of those people who is galvanized by crisis. Stress, difficulty, some insurmountable obstacle: it brings out the best in them.

Me, it brings out nothing but soap and water.

Not washing for several hours, level of distress: about 150. Off the charts.

"Let's go up and check on Stella," Anthony says.

"You go ahead," I say. "I'm just going to use the bathroom. I'll meet you out front." I try to sound casual, like all I'm going to do is pee, wash my hands once like I'm supposed to, and leave. I'd like to wait until I get home to my own bathroom sink, but I'm too agitated. I'll wash here, in the germy hospital. At least they'll have antibacterial soap.

"Okay," Anthony says. "But do me a favor."

"What," I say, knowing what it is.

"Don't wash."

"I'm not sure I can do that."

"I'm sure," he says. "Promise me?"

"I don't always keep my promises." Here I am, telling him another secret. Soon I'll be spilling my guts to this guy. I tell lies, I'll say. In fourth grade, I let a boy cheat off me in math. My mother is an alcoholic and my whole life I have tried, and failed, to please her enough. I think about killing myself probably more than the average person.

"Keep this one," he says.

48.

JAMIE flips her wallet open and pushes it across the bar to show her fake ID to the bartender.

"California," the bartender says. "That's where I'm from. I really miss it."

"Not me," Jamie says. When her White Russian arrives, she takes it back to the table where Leila and her friends are sitting. Earlier, Jamie watched them in rehearsal, onstage in an auditorium empty of any audience except Jamie. Everyone focused on their moves, serious and concentrated. She loved watching Leila dance. For about the thousandth time, she wished she had a talent, any talent, that would make people look at her and admire her.

I'm nobody, Jamie thinks. I don't have any money and I don't know how to do anything.

"Jay-*mee,*" Leila's friend Chris says. "Come sit next to me." Chris is the only one who isn't a dancer; he's studying playwriting. One of his instructors wrote a play that Kathleen Turner acted in. Leila told Jamie all about Chris. "Don't flirt with him, he's mine," Leila had said.

"So what do you do out in California?" Chris says. "Are you going to school, or what?"

Jamie takes a big sip of her drink. Hasn't Leila told Chris about her? Jamie has told Diana all about Leila. Doesn't Leila ever talk about her best friend? Are they even best friends any-more? Right now Leila is laughing with Naima. Naima, who is a beautiful black girl with an amazing body and fluid, graceful movements. Watching her dance earlier in her skin-tight leo-tard, Jamie could see that her stomach was completely flat. Naima has probably never been with a boy without making him use a condom. Her parents are probably artists of some kind with a penthouse on the Upper West Side. Naima sings as well as dances, Leila said. Naima is going to be in an off-Broadway musical. Good for her. Jamie hates her already.

"Or what?" Chris says. "I've always wanted to go to Califor-nia."

"I'm not doing much right now," Jamie says. "I kind of thought I'd move here. Get a job, work on some creative stuff."

"Awesome," Chris says. "I'm writing a play right now. A one-act. It all takes place in a men's bathroom."

"I always wondered what you guys do in there."

"There are three characters. Two of them are gay, and one is a cop. The thing is, the cop is one of the gay guys."

"I don't get it." Leila is still laughing with Naima. Jamie wishes they would shut up. Now Dakota, a tiny girl with long pink and blond dreadlocks, leans toward them to share the joke.

"These two guys are having sex in the bathroom, and the cop comes in," Chris says. "Only, one guy having the sex is really straight. He's, like, a male prostitute and just has sex for money. So the gay cop comes in, only nobody knows he's gay, not even him, at first."

"Sounds great," Jamie says. Maybe she is gay and doesn't know it, and that's why she feels so jealous right now watching Leila with Naima and Dakota. Maybe she should just become a lesbian in her new life. Girls do it all the time, give up boys and switch over. How hard can it be? In junior high she'd had a friend named Caroline, and they used to draw on each other's naked backs with their forefingers. They spelled out the names of boys they liked, or words the other one had to guess, or hearts and horses. Whenever Caroline drew on her back, Jamie had a warm liquid feeling that flowed through all her limbs, and she felt bereft when Caroline erased everything with the palm of her hand and pulled her shirt down and said, "Now you do me." Jamie and Leila had kissed a couple of times, once just pressing their lips on each other's in freshman year and then, in sophomore year, using their tongues. It had felt great. Leila's lips were soft, softer than any boy's. No wonder Leila had boys after her all the time, wanting to kiss her. I can find a rich older woman, Jamie thinks, and she'll support me.

I need a plan, and I don't have one.

I could make clothes, I know it.

On *Lifetime: Intimate Biography* there are always stories of stars who struggled through poverty and hard times before becoming famous. It all makes sense when you look at it backward, from the vantage point of their current situation: the Beverly Hills or Malibu home, the gold records on the wall or Oscar statuettes on the mantel. Once they were fucked up and anorexic, pillheads or coke freaks or alcohol abusers, losers who even then were glamorous because one day they were going to become the sexy people you stare at on magazine covers, dressed in cool clothes, gazing at you while little sparks of light glitter in the center of their pupils. It's like their present perfection casts this bright light back into every dark corner. But how do you go forward from being a loser? It's a secret Jamie doesn't know. Leila seems to know how to move toward her life. Her friends, too—they have an idea where they're going.

"That guy is checking you out," Leila says, turning away from Naima and Dakota, giving Jamie a little nudge with her shoulder.

"Where?" Jamie says.

"Third from the left, at the bar."

Jamie looks. "He's not."

"He was."

Just then he cocks his head and gives her a sidelong glance. And he's cute. Definitely cute. Cocoa-colored skin, a nearly shaved head covered by just a shadow of black stubble. He's got a nicely shaped head.

"Dare you to go over there," Leila says.

"No way," Jamie says.

The guy keeps looking, and smiles. Only one side of his mouth goes up; it's a smirk, but an appealing one. She can tell that if she went over, he'd be glad.

Maybe she can be a prostitute. They could go have sex in the alley, and she could walk back into the bar with some cash in her pocket. There are lots of options for eighteen-year-old girls, now that she thinks about it. Stripper. Lap dancer. Nude model. Whore. She could get a webcam and broadcast images of herself doing whatever—taking a shower, washing dishes, peeing. That would probably be enough, without even having to masturbate or have sex with anybody.

"Double dare you," Leila says.

"I can't." The truth is, Jamie is too shy. She could never take her clothes off in front of people, even invisible people somewhere in cyberspace. She can't even go over to that cute boy. He's still looking at her, waiting for her to get up from the table and saunter over. She's not going to. Let him come to her, if he thinks she's that hot.

He doesn't, though. He turns back to his beer, and then starts talking to a guy on his left, who looks over at her for an instant. They are probably laughing at her, talking about what a dog she is. The guy on the left probably bet his friend he could get Jamie to walk over there. Boys are such assholes.

Leila's cell phone sings out the opening notes of Beethoven's

"Ode to Joy." Leila's phone is translucent shocking pink. It takes pictures, and does about a million other things.

"This is Leila," she says. Pause. "Hi, Mrs. Ramirez." Pause. "As a matter of fact, I do know where she is. Just a minute." She holds the phone out to Jamie. "Your mother," she says. "You might want to take it outside, I can hardly hear her."

Jamie takes the phone and walks toward the door. The tables are so close together she has to go up past the bar to get there. When she passes the cute guy and his friend, neither one of them even turns around. She goes out through the saloon doors. She's wearing jeans and a sweater Leila loaned her, but she feels the chill of the brick wall against her back when she leans against it.

"Mom," she says.

"I am stunned," her mother says. "I am truly stunned."

"Why are you calling me? How did you get Leila's number?"

"You had it written on your mirror."

"Mom, you're not supposed to go in my room."

"It's not your room, if you're living at Diana's. She was here. Anthony was here."

I should have left a message with Diana, Jamie thinks. *Take care of Stella. Tell her I'm sorry. Tell her I wasn't fit to be her mother.* It never occurred to her that Diana would go to her mother's house, looking for her. Shit.

"She's in the hospital," her mother says.

"Diana? What happened to her?"

Her mother sighs. "Honey," she says. "Your daughter is in the hospital. You had better come home now."

Jamie closes her eyes. She opens them and sees a New Yorker in a ragged black raincoat and shoes that are too big for him. A homeless New Yorker, picking through some New York garbage for bottles to sell. He has a nylon shoulder bag through which she can see a few cans and bottles he's already collected.

"Jamie?" her mother says. "Did you hear what I said?"

"I freaked out," Jamie says.

"They're keeping her for observation, but they think she's going to be all right. She gave everyone quite a scare."

"Why do you keep saying 'she'?" Jamie says. "She has a name, you know."

"Yes, I know. I know that you are not behaving responsibly here."

"Stella Maricela Ramirez." Maricela was Jamie's Mexican grandmother's name.

"Do you have money for a plane ticket?"

"No."

"Borrow it from Leila. I'll pay her back."

"Okay," Jamie says. "Okay. I'm coming as soon as I can. I'm sorry, Mom," she says, starting to cry. "I'm so sorry."

"With crisis comes opportunity," her mother says, and for once, Jamie doesn't feel like gagging at her mother's New Age wisdom. Well, maybe a little. That's not important now.

"I'll see you soon," Jamie says. She heads back inside, not seeing the boy at the bar, the crowded tables, not seeing anything in New York. She doesn't belong in New York. She goes up to Leila and hands her the phone.

"What happened?" Leila says.

Everyone is looking at her. She picks up a napkin from the table and wipes her eyes. A feeling of calm comes over her.

"My daughter," she says, "is sick. I'm afraid I have to go."

49.

STELLA likes the hospital. She's getting lots of attention. All these faces leaning over her, soft hands stroking her arm, a pleasant beeping sound coming from a heart monitor. *Blip blip blip.* A teddy bear is next to her, not the one she's used to but another one, smaller and bright pink, with a white bow tie around his neck. A perfectly fine teddy bear. "Hi sweetheart," the nurses say. "Hey, little one. Stella, honey. Hello, darling girl." It's one big love fest at this hospital.

And Eva is here somewhere. Eva's memories are growing lighter and brighter like overexposed film, but Stella can still see them. She closes her eyes and sees a river going by. She puts her whole face in it, looking for Eva.

She can feel her. There's a wavery image, or just the outlines of one. Anthony is weeping by the bed, his face in his hands, his shoulders shaking. But Anthony was driving Diana's car, driving fast toward the hospital, not crying at all. That's good. Eva had watched him at her funeral. He was standing in front of her casket, at a tall podium, trying to say a few words. Sun came in through stained glass, watery red and blue light. Anthony's parents were there. And Eva's parents—her father looking straight ahead, her mother sobbing, curled up in the pew. Her students from Sidwell Friends, her music students—practically everyone was crying. Anthony was trying to speak but he couldn't get past his own sobs. A woman in a black pantsuit came up, put her arm around his shoulders and led him to a seat. Eva couldn't leave him. Not like that. She had turned out to be as bad as him, holding on, not wanting to let him go. She floated in the river, but now something is happening. The river is starting to go dry. Wait. There's warmth between her legs. Water.

Blip blip blip. She has to pee, and does. She's breathing. Air goes in. Her name is Eva. No, the nurses said something else. It was so hard to hear them. Their voices grew fainter and fainter. Now they're gone.

My name is, my name is.

Blip blip blip.

50.

REMEMBER: Each time you view your experiences as a test, you set yourself up for disappointment, discouragement, self-criticism, and resignation.

I WASHED in the bathroom of the emergency room for at least five minutes. At Mary Wagner-Ramirez's house, I went into the bathroom where the plants grew and washed my hands, and my arms up to the shoulders, while Anthony sat in the living room sipping green tea and filling her in on Stella's situation and Jamie's absence. Now we are back at my apartment, and I am taking a shower. I'm thinking I've got to move again. Someplace the air isn't full of salt and gull shit and dust, someplace I will not have to touch doorknobs or use public bathrooms. I scrub myself from head to foot with water as hot as I can stand it. My skin is red and raw and I don't see how things are ever going to be any different.

"Diana?" It's Anthony, knocking on the door. "Time to quit now. You're clean."

"Go away," I call. He shouldn't be anywhere near the master bathroom. No one is allowed in here. This and the bedroom are the only safe places left.

"If you don't come out," he says, "I'm coming in."

"Don't you dare. Don't come in here."

But the next minute he's opened the door. I can see him through the shower glass, a blurry form taking off his clothes.

"Get out, get out!" I'm screaming now. "I don't even know you!"

He slides the shower door open, and steps onto the tiles. There he is. A naked man, a man I met just last night, reaching for the soap in my hand.

"Anthony," I say. "What are you doing?"

"I don't know. What am I doing? Showering, I think. I didn't get a chance to, earlier. You woke me out of a sound sleep to drag me to the hospital."

I look at his body. A man's body, tan and muscular. The tattoo on his chest is, as I suspected, a heart. A red heart with a scroll across the center, the name "Eva" in script written on the scroll. It's like she's in here with us.

He's taken off the chain with the wedding rings, I notice. Maybe he just uses it as a way to pick up women in bars. There is black hair sprouting through the heart on his chest, starting to flatten from the spray of the water. There is a little hair on his belly, and again below his navel, a thick line of black hair leading down to his—

Okay, you can picture the rest.

"Let me get under the shower," he says. "I'll soap you."

I hand him the soap, then move to the far end of the shower. Of course, I don't touch the shower walls, or the sliding glass door. I cross my arms over my breasts and hunch forward, while he tips his head back to the jets of water from the shower head. He closes his eyes and runs his hands through his black hair, and I have to say, I feel something that is not completely revulsion. But still, he is a strange man who has invaded a very sacred space, a space only Tim and I have ever been in. He soaps himself all over, quickly, and rinses off.

"Come here," he says.

I move closer, and he lathers the soap by rubbing it between his wet palms.

"Raise your arms," he says.

"Left one first," I say, and he obliges, rubbing the soap in slow circles under my left armpit, moving down my arm. "Now right."

But instead he keeps going, down my left side. Breast, waist, hip.

"This is all wrong," I say.

"Hush." He finishes my left side, kneeling down to lift my foot. I have to put my hand on his shoulder to steady myself. He soaps each toe, just like I do. Then he stands up and starts on my right side, and when he's done with that he lathers up his hands again. "Turn around," he says. He runs one hand down between my legs, from front to back, and I nearly faint. Next I feel his hands on my shoulders, massaging them as much as washing them. I close my eyes and try to remember the last time Tim, or anyone, gave me a massage.

"Done," he says. "Now rinse and get out." He steps out and grabs a towel.

I rinse—a long rinse—and then step onto the rug. He hands me the towel he's just finished using, and picks up his jeans from the toilet lid—the ones he's just taken off. The dirty ones, in other words.

I look at the towel. "I need a—a dry one."

"This will have to do."

I take it. I pat myself with it, rather than rub. Anthony stands there watching me, holding his jeans in one hand, making no move to put them on. I wonder what he thinks of me naked. I am sure my naked body looks nothing like Eva's—Eva with her delicate stick legs and big sensual hands. My legs are rounded, the calves well-defined from all the ballet classes Gloria made me take when I was little. My hands are still a child's hands, dry

and small. My breasts are large and no longer perky. I bet Eva
had small, high breasts, elegant breasts that would never have
dropped, never shown the striation of a single stretch mark, if
she had lived.

Anthony looks at me, and he starts to get hard. We both look
down at his penis, like it's something that has wandered into the
bathroom, something that has disturbed us during a private moment.

I wonder if he is going to tell me to go into the bedroom, if
he is going to follow me in there, and I don't know if I want him
to or not.

"Diana," he says. "I'm not ready."

"That makes two of us," I say.

I wait for the romantic moment, the one where one of us
says, "We can't do this. This is wrong." Then we clutch at each
other like animals, gasping and moaning. We are larger than life-
size. In a dark movie theater, girls stare at us and eat too much
buttered popcorn, then go home and look at their bodies in the
mirror and hate themselves.

Anthony drops his jeans on the floor. The *floor.*

He pulls his shirt off a towel rack and starts to button it. The
front of the shirt covers his penis, but I can see it's still hard. "I'll
check on Stella this afternoon," he says, "and call you when I
hear anything. Jamie's mother wants to take the baby home
with her."

"Okay," I say.

"She was going to try and reach Jamie's friend."

"Leila. That's good." I'm talking to his penis, watching it go
down, watching it disappear.

"Mary seems to have had a change of heart. She's been very
angry at Jamie. I think she's been angry about everything. Her
husband's condition, especially."

"That's wonderful. I mean, about the change of heart." I hear what he's saying: Stella will be with Mary Wagner-Ramirez. Jamie, if she hasn't been raped and murdered, or run off to Mexico, will probably be with Mary, too. Anthony will be welcome in their tiled home, and will visit often. I will be alone again.

"'Bye, then," Anthony says, picking up his jeans and putting them on. No underwear. No concern about how those jeans have been in that germ-filled hospital. No problem letting them touch the floor, then his body.

He puts a hand out and cups my cheek. Anthony's hands are big, just like Eva's were. I understand clearly that he and Eva were a matched set. I close my eyes for a second and think, This is how he must have touched Eva, this is what it felt like to be his wife. And I envy her, poor dead Eva, who got to feel this.

"See you," Anthony says, and goes.

I wait to hear the front door click behind him. He had no reason to stay, really. No reason to come back, either. I can move away and forget this whole stupid episode in my life. No more depressed teenaged mothers, no more babies wailing in the middle of the night. I'll get a new job and impress everyone with my diligence. I'll avoid all contamination.

But I know there's only one real way to avoid it. Eva's brother knew what to do, but I can't see hanging myself. When you hang, you convulse, your blood vessels rupture. With a gun, your brains spill everywhere. Drink poison, and you vomit and froth at the mouth. Pills are definitely the answer.

I can get Valium in Mexico, like Tim did. Find a pharmacy in Tijuana. Get as clean a hotel room as possible and take the whole bottle, along with some tequila. I'll leave a note for my mother: *'Bye, Mom. Life was too hard.* I won't call her Gloria.

I'll put rose petals on the bed and drift off, surrounded by roses, and that will be the end of all this.

51.

JAMIE has a feeling of panic as she gets on the plane. Something could happen: faulty hydraulics, a terrorist hijacking. She will never see her baby again. She looks at the—the male stewardess—what are they called, anyway? Stewards? *Flight attendants.* That's what they're called. Her mother still says words like "stewardess." The flight attendant, a small man with greased black hair, smiles at her, but she can tell he doesn't mean it. He looks like he wants to be a million miles away from this plane and everyone in it. Maybe he knows something. The plane is too old, or the mechanics are sitting around stoned instead of triple-checking all the things that could go wrong. Or the pilot has a drinking problem. The flight attendant smiles his fake smile and nods at Jamie. "Hi," he says. She ignores him and heads for her seat. A window seat, so she can look out and not talk to anyone.

She slips her purse under the seat in front of her. She opens the *Harper's Bazaar* she bought at the airport, the Fall Fashion Issue, Madonna on the cover. She flips through the zillion ads at the front of the magazine, before the table of contents. A four-page spread for Estée Lauder, then Prada, Armani, Dior. Lancôme. The Gucci ad has a black model, in black leather, and at her hip is a beautiful brown baby. The model's got a white bag slung over her left shoulder, presumably the Gucci part of the ad. Her right hand cradles the baby's ass. Jamie wonders if the baby is really the model's child, or just borrowed as a prop. She keeps flipping pages, to take her mind off the sound of the jet engines starting up, the push back from the gate, the turn as they taxi out onto the runway. There are ten whole pages filled with a gorgeous blonde posing for Calvin Klein. I want those boots, Jamie thinks. I want those jeans, that hair, those lips.

"I hate flying," a boy next to her says. He's maybe thirteen, fourteen—she can see a little dark, downy hair on his upper lip, that he's probably proud of. He's got a white iPod on his lap.

She wants that iPod.

"Ever since 9/11," he says, "it totally tweaks me."

"I know what you mean," Jamie says.

"Airport security is bullshit," the boy says. "Did you hear about the kid who flew around with a bunch of box cutters, just to show the airlines how easily somebody could do it?"

"I think so."

The boy is chewing gum rapidly. The plane hasn't taken off yet; they're just sitting on the runway, waiting for their turn.

"Got any more gum?" Jamie says.

"Sure." He leans over, reaches into a pocket of his backpack under the seat, and comes up with a pack of Dentyne.

"Every time I get on a plane?" the boy says. "I find myself looking at every guy who might be Arab. Any guy with dark hair and a dark beard. There's always one who looks suspicious to me. Then I just watch him, and if he does anything weird, like keeps looking around the cabin, I'm convinced he's the one who's going to blow up the plane with the explosives in his shoes."

"Where are you going?" Jamie says, to distract him. She doesn't want to hear about terrorists.

"Home," the boy says. "I was supposed to live with my dad this year, in Park Slope, but it wasn't working out. So it's back to Mom. It sucks, 'cause school already started. Now I get to go back to my old school, but I'll be behind."

"Why didn't it work out?"

"My dad's a dick," the boy says matter-of-factly. "He never wanted me in the first place. My mom had to talk him into taking me, and then when I got there he was, like, so lame. It was like, 'Make yourself some dinner.' 'Here's some money, go buy some stuff for school.' How did I know where to buy stuff? I didn't know which buses to take or anything."

"That sucks," Jamie says.

"Plus, I missed my mom," the boy says.

The engines have grown louder. The plane starts down the runway with a roar, going faster and faster.

"This is the part I hate," the boy says. "I mean, I know if the terrorists are going to do anything, it won't be until we're in the air. But this is like the last stop before the air. Once we're up there, anything could happen."

"Yeah, anything could happen," Jamie says. She takes the boy's hand. He's just a scared little kid. He's more afraid than she is, and she knows what to do.

The boy closes his eyes. He squeezes her hand as they lift off the ground.

52

WHERE are we?
      In the hospital.

I don't want to die. I want to be with Anthony.

You have to go back now.

I'm so tired . . . I don't want to go.

You can go. I'm here now.

The water evaporates. Eva is mist, then air, then nothing.
Stella reaches out toward the nothing. The Light is inside the
nothing, or is it the other way around? She doesn't know anymore. The Light was so long ago. Even the Before has grown so
fuzzy in her memory. That pulsing that was her whole being,
now it's just her heart beating.

Blip, blip, blip.

The Before, what was that?

Stella looks at the nurses. She waves her arms around. A rubber nipple is put into her mouth, and warm formula comes
through it, sweet and rich.

"Stella, Stella," the nurses say.

Stella drinks in big gulps. For a couple of minutes she fights
to stay awake, and then she lets go, falling into sleep.

53.

HOMEWORK: Ask your friends and family
for help.

A S soon as Anthony leaves, I have the urge to get back in the shower. It's not an overwhelming urge, though. I try some Calming Breaths.

Surprise: they work. Sort of. I wash my hands once. The phone rings while I'm putting on clean clothes. By the time I get to it, Gloria is saying good-bye. "Hello, hello," I say. "Gloria?"

"Oh, good, you're there."

"What is it? What's wrong?"

"You always think something's wrong," she says. "Nothing's wrong."

"I don't see how you can say that."

"Honey, nothing's wrong with my life. Yours is the one that's troubled."

"Gloria," I say, "has anyone ever told you you're an alcoholic?" I don't know where that came from. Certainly I've never told her, all these years.

"All the time," she says cheerfully. "I'm highly functioning, though."

So much for that conversation. "Why did you call, Gloria?"

"They've found a little something," she says.

"They? Who?"

"The doctors. It's nothing. I go for a few sessions where they drip some fluid into me for a few hours, and that's it."

"Cancer. You're saying you have cancer."

"It's just a little thing. I shouldn't have told you. You're such a worrier."

"Where is it?"

"Where is what?"

For God's sake. "The cancer. Where is the cancer?"

"Never mind about that. That's not why I called. I wanted to tell you I read up on your disease. Fred got me a book from the library."

"Fred left his vibrating chair?" I say. "Fred went to the library?"

"Here's the trick," she says. "This book says it's like being in the jungle. The lion is roaring, and you have to go toward it."

"I want to talk about *your* disease," I say.

"I want you to call that doctor you were seeing."

"Maybe. I don't know. I don't know what I'm going to do."

I see myself on a bed in a hotel room in Tijuana, surrounded by roses. The roses have shriveled and blackened. I lie there, looking and smelling disgusting, princess of nothing. I'm a little Day of the Dead figure, a skeleton with a bit of cotton fluff for hair, lying in a glassed-in box on a crude wooden bed.

"You used to count all the time, when you were little," Gloria says. "I remember thinking it was strange, sometimes. I should have realized."

"You should have realized a lot of things," I say. "You should have realized that there was more to me than my looks, or some stupid dance routine. You were as bad as one of those pageant judges, rating me on everything. And you still do that, Gloria. You still judge me."

I can't believe I'm saying all this. The more things I say to her, the more my skin crawls, but I can't stop. "You have to stop judging me," I say.

I realize I do not want to be Princess of the Dead. I don't even want to be Sleeping Beauty, comatose in her palace, waiting for the prince to come though the thorns and brambles to find me.

"I'm sorry, baby," she says.

"I'm not your baby."

"Oh, you'll always be my baby. You'll understand that one day, when you have children of your own."

"I don't want children. And don't you say anything about that."

"Promise me you'll see that doctor again," Gloria says.

"Promise me you won't die."

She snorts. "Jesus H. Christ," she says. "You're not getting rid of me that easily."

"I don't want to get rid of you."

"Have I been too hard on you?" Gloria says. "Have I?"

I hesitate. Then I say, "In a word? Yes."

"Well, I never made much of myself. I was hoping you'd have a chance."

"What, to be on *Star Search*? I don't want to be a model, Gloria. I don't want to be a famous actress, or a pop diva. I just want—" I stop. I don't know what it is I want.

I want to get better.

If I can.

"I want what everybody wants," I say. "To be happy. To live in a world that makes sense."

"I want that for you," she says.

"Mom," I say.

"What?"

"I miss you," I tell her. "Do you miss me?"

"Every minute," she says.

54.

JAMIE steps onto the sidewalk at Long Beach Airport just as her mom pulls up in the Honda.

"Hi," Jamie says, getting in. Brown rosary beads swing from the rearview and settle. "I'm sorry, Mom," she says. "God, I am so sorry."

"It's my fault, too," her mom says. "I should have helped you. I don't know why I was so punishing."

Jamie wants to put her arms around her, but they are on the road now. She remembers how they used to make up from fights when she was little: "It's my fault," Jamie would say. "No, it's *my* fault," her mom would say. Then they would hug each other. They couldn't stay mad at each other for long.

"You wanted me to learn responsibility," Jamie says.

"There are days," her mom says, "when I just want to pack it in and split. I imagine getting in the car and driving to New Mexico, renting a little adobe house in the Sangre de Cristos. Just me and the cat. Fuck all this," her mom says. "It's too goddamned difficult."

"Where's Stella? Is she okay?"

"They're releasing her this afternoon. I'll take you over there to pick her up."

Jamie touches her shoulder. "How's Dad?"

"He looks at me, and I know he sees me," her mom says. "I know he's in there."

"Of course he is," Jamie says, though she's not sure, herself, that it's true. She rubs her mom's shoulder. "He's going to get better. It's just a slow process."

"Hell's bells," her mom says. "Who knows? Not me. I'm just hanging on from day to day."

They get to the house and her mom stops at the curb. "I'm dropping you off," she says. "I've got to get some groceries. I didn't want to leave your father alone for too long."

"I can watch him."

"See if you can get some soup in him. There's a pot in the fridge you can heat up."

Walking in the front door feels weird to Jamie; it's like she's home, but not. It's all familiar, but she doesn't quite fit anymore. She takes a deep breath of sandalwood, listens to the five-note chimes ringing on the porch behind her as she steps into the foyer.

"Dad?" she calls.

He's sleeping on the couch, on his back, an afghan thrown over him. Light is coming in from the panes of glass at the top of the front door, falling softly on his face. The weave of the couch is pressed into one cheek, like he was lying on his side and has just turned over. His mouth is open. He looks like he did when she would come into her parents' room at night, still wanting to sleep with them, when they said she was too old and had to be a big girl and sleep alone. Her dad would be lying like that, sound asleep, and she'd shake him awake and whisper.

"Can I sleep with you guys?"

He would roll over, open his eyes, smile at her. "No, sweetheart. Go back to bed. You'll be all right."

"But I'm scared."

"I'll tuck you in." He would take her back to bed. "Nothing to be scared of. We're right down the hall."

She touches his shoulder. "Dad?" she says.

He opens his eyes and looks at her.

"Hi, Daddy," she says. "I'm back." She waits for him to say something, for some strange word to fly out of him. But he just looks at her. Then he smiles, a wide, blissful smile that makes his whole face scrunch up and his eyes almost disappear, the kind of smile she imagines an insane person having.

"Do you want some soup?" Jamie says.

He nods, still smiling.

"That's good," Jamie says. "Let me get that for you."

She goes into the kitchen, finds the pot and sets it on the stove, turns on the burner underneath it. Then she runs back to the living room. "You nodded," she says to him. "You understand what I'm saying, right?"

His head doesn't move. Maybe it was a spasm, an involuntary motion.

"Of course you do," she says.

55.

GOAL #1: Seek out uncertainty.

AFTER I hang up with Gloria, I dial Teddy's World.

"Teddy's World, where babies are our business," Marlene says.

"Marlene, it's me."

"Where have you been?" Marlene says. "No call, nothing. I've been here wondering all morning. I left you three messages."

"I had an emergency," I say. Maybe if I tell her the emergency concerned a baby, she will understand. Then again, Marlene doesn't really like babies, any more than I do. She told me so once. If I told her about showering with Anthony, that would interest her. But I am not going to. I am not even going to think about it.

"I need to know I can depend on you, Diana," Marlene says. "If you're going to keep this job."

"Marlene," I say, "you know damned well you can depend on me. If I say it was an emergency, it was. Now I've got some things to deal with, and I'm taking the day off. See you tomorrow." Then I hang up.

Marlene is not going to fire me. Employees of the Month do not get fired. They may leave of their own accord, but no one shows them the door. And I am not going to leave. I'm going to ask Marlene for a raise, and she's going to bitch and moan, and then she's going to give it to me.

The phone rings again.

For a second, I hope it's Tim. I imagine telling him I'm going to get better, really get better this time.

It's Anthony. "What are you doing?" he says. "I want to see you."

"You left less than an hour ago."

"I forgot something."

I try to think what he could have left behind. His sunglasses. His underwear. He just pulled up those dirty jeans.

"So what did you forget?"

"I lost my earring."

The diamond stud. I walk back to the bathroom to look for it. "My mother has cancer," I tell him.

"I'm sorry," he says.

"She says it's nothing. Can it be nothing?"

"Sometimes. It's not always a death sentence, you know."

"Life is a death sentence," I say. Then, because it sounds so good, I say it again.

"Yeah, but there's the meantime."

"Anthony, I don't want her to die."

"Death is the mother of beauty," he says.

"That's Wallace Stevens," I say, thrilled I can name the poet. I wonder if Eva would know it. She'd probably be able to quote the whole poem. "Sunday Morning," it's called. All I remember is that one famous line, and something from the end, about birds going down into darkness. "Is that supposed to comfort me?" I say.

"I don't know. All I know is that we're alive, now. I'm sorry about your mother."

I'm in the bathroom, looking into the shower. There's a black hair curled by the drain.

"Okay, I'm at your door down here," Anthony says. "Can you buzz me up?"

"I thought you were at your place."

"No, no, I'm calling on my cell."

Anthony is downstairs. I should tell him to go away. I think of how he looked, naked, standing in my shower. How he threw his head back, enjoying it.

I look around the bathroom. This is where he stood—a strange man, naked. This is where his jeans lay on the rug.

"Diana?" Anthony says on the phone. "Let's go for a ride. Let's go to the desert."

"Why?"

"Because we can look at the sky without thermal inversion. I've got roast chicken sandwiches, and tortilla chips and salsa. Cheese and apples. We can sit on a blanket and picnic, and when it's night we can look at the stars."

I think about the desert. Sagebrush and cactus and thin, dizzying air. Dirt. Lizards sliding on their bellies, snakes crawling around and shedding their skin. "I hate nature," I say. "The desert is dry. It's dusty."

"No, it's pure."

"I don't even know you." Just because I let you in my shower, I'm thinking. Not that that isn't a big thing.

A huge thing, in fact.

"Maybe you do," Anthony says. "Maybe you know me."

"I don't. I have no idea who you are. You're some guy who lost his wife. I feel sorry for you, I do. But I have my own problems."

"Yeah, we're your basic fucked-up human beings," he says.

"I don't want to know you," I say.

"Yes, you do. Come on, it's just a drive."

"I thought you gave your car away."

"We're taking yours. I walked over carrying this stuff. Come on, let me in."

"I'll come down," I say.

I click off the phone and stand looking in the bathroom mirror for a minute. Thinking, I should put on some makeup. Thinking, I could go out the back way, by the beach, and wait there until he leaves.

There's Eva's earring, a little bright gleam on the navy bathroom rug. The back that holds the stud in place is on the floor under the sink. I kneel on the rug to pick up the earring. I think of how it's been in Anthony's ear, then on the floor, but I slip it in anyway, through the hole in my left ear where I haven't worn anything for a year or so. I had a little infection so I stopped wearing earrings entirely. Even after my ear healed I didn't start again. I just got out of the habit, I guess. The hole has closed a bit but I can push the earring through.

I am not going to be able to replace her, I know. But maybe there is something else. Lying in her hospital bed, maybe Eva, at the end, sat up through the haze of pain and morphine. Maybe she took this out of her ear, and put it in Anthony's palm and closed his fingers around it. Knowing he would wear it, knowing one day he wouldn't have to anymore.

I put the back part on to hold the earring, and then I go into the bedroom. I sit on the edge of my bed. I can hear traffic outside, the world going about its business, the messy world that at this moment doesn't include me. Out there people are working and arguing and laughing, living their beautiful, terrible lives, falling in love and having babies and being bored out of their skulls and feeling depressed, then being consoled by some little thing like watching the patterns the light makes through the leaves of trees, casting shadows on the sidewalks.

I remember the line from that poem now.

Downward to darkness, on extended wings.

I sit there another minute, in the middle of my perfectly clean room, as still as a doll on a shelf. Then I go get my jacket, in case the desert gets cold at night.

About the Author

Kim Addonizio has published several collections of poetry including *Tell Me,* a finalist for the 2000 National Book Award, and, most recently *What Is This Thing Called Love.* With Dorianne Laux, she coauthored *The Poet's Companion: A Guide to the Pleasures of Writing Poetry.* Her poems and stories have appeared widely, and her work has been honored with two National Endowment for the Arts fellowships, a Guggenheim fellowship, a Pushcart Prize, and the Mississippi Review Fiction Prize. She lives in Oakland, California, and is online at http://addonizio.home.mindspring.com.